TAKE

THE

MIC

FICTIONAL STORIES OF
EVERYDAY RESISTANCE

EDITED BY BETHANY C. MORROW

TAKE

FICTIONAL STORIES OF EVERYDAY RESISTANCE

THE
MIC

EDITED
BY
BETHANY C.
MORROW

ARTHUR A. LEVINE BOOKS
AN IMPRINT OF SCHOLASTIC INC.

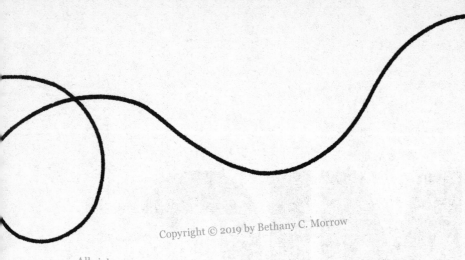

Library of Congress Cataloging-in-Publication Data available

ISBN 978-1-338-34370-0

10 9 8 7 6 5 4 3 2 1   19 20 21 22 23

Printed in the U. S. A. 23
First edition, October 2019

Book design by Baily Crawford

FOR MY EZRA, WHO KNOWS HIS
WAY AROUND A MICROPHONE. YOU
MAKE ME PROUD, AND I HOPE I CAN
RETURN THE FAVOR.

– BCM

TABLE OF CONTENTS

INTRODUCTION

WHEN I WAS FIRST ASKED to write a pitch for an anthology featuring "stories that show the power of resistance against systems of oppression," I didn't know what to write. Writing is part of my existence, but for years I'd felt like it was drying up. While Black men and women and children were killed in the street, or in their cars, or in the park, or in their own apartments, I felt a piece of me shriveling up. Dehydrating. Like my blood was running with theirs. I'd never experienced anything like it. I felt out of time and space some, the way you do when the world stops making sense. It couldn't be real, I thought, or else I couldn't be.

But it kept happening. And I kept losing pieces of myself.

The morning of the 2017 presidential inauguration, I finally started writing. I was only being asked for a pitch at that point, but I started drafting my short story, "As You Were." I wrote about a Black girl slaying in her marching band drill down for several reasons. Firstly because marching band is life. (S/O Mighty Matadors Marching Band! Never forget!) But more importantly, as a man with a documented and observable history of bigotry, prejudice, and misogyny was being sworn into the highest office in the land, I felt both hopeless about the unrelenting force of systemic oppression against my people and increasingly convinced that I would not tolerate a single instance more of interpersonal insult. Something about that conviction — and maybe about the fact that I could still feel it — made some part inside me tingle, as if it could potentially come back to life. So I mean it when I say existence, simply continuing to exist in the face of overt, unrelenting oppression, is a form of resistance.

I thought of the many ways teenage years involve feeling out of control, especially before you even have the option of voting. But I thought too of all the times I'd felt offended, confused, and silent, in the company of so-called friends. I thought about the death by a million cuts young marginalized people often suffer that marching in an organized protest doesn't really alleviate or address. And I thought about the danger of telling Black kids — in a country that had been engaged in a kind of one-sided civil war, in a campaign against our lives and bodies, in which our killers are time and time again acquitted — that the only real resistance was the kind that is far more physically dangerous to them in particular. I won't try to dissuade a young activist from taking to the street in organized resistance, but I also won't ever tell a marginalized kid that they aren't resisting, that they aren't struggling, that their continuing on isn't enough. Not when their classmates are using law enforcement to play practical jokes on them, completely ignorant of the trauma and mental unwellness that comes with having an abundance of proof that your life can be taken, and you could be blamed. A real-life phenomenon that inspired my story. Not when their human rights are up for debate, as in the stories by Darcie Little Badger and Ray Stoeve. Not when their communities are trying to force self-denial and assimilation on them, as in another real-life-inspired story by Yamile Saied Méndez.

I knew from the start that I wanted this anthology to be about the everyday. I wanted not only to acknowledge the more dangerous world in which you are growing up, but to give you permission to resist everywhere. Not just in the street, against an obvious foe, but also in your lives, in your schools, in your friendships. I wanted to give you stories of kids who might not have control of their country, but who take control of the moments that make up their reality.

An Indigenous girl who doesn't stand for unwanted physical advances ("Grace," by Darcie Little Badger).

A Jewish girl who calls out anti-Semitism, whether in the form of online vitriol or casual prejudice from a close friend ("Ruth," by Laura Silverman).

A Muslimah who won't answer every offensive interrogation that normalized Islamophobia allows ("Are You the Good Kind of Muslim?" by Samira Ahmed).

My hope is that *Take the Mic* will act as both a call and a comfort. To own those smaller, less visible acts of resistance that aren't getting news coverage, and to tell you that you are not going unnoticed. You are not forgotten.

Keep going.

Keep living, keep loving yourselves and each other.

We're proud of you, and we're going to keep fighting to make you proud of us.

Bethany C. Morrow

GRACE

BY DARCIE LITTLE BADGER

WHEN I WAS VERY YOUNG, Mama taught me three things.

One. Someday, we'll go home. It's there, waiting, never really stolen. But until then, we gotta live like a pair of dandelion fluffs in the wind and drift around until the day comes to settle and grow.

Two. I'm alive because my great-grandma, great-great-grandma, and great-great-great-grandma resisted the men who tried to round them up and kill them or steal everything that mattered. Even when it meant hiding in plain sight, surviving in small enclaves after the world figured we all died. It hadn't always been that way. Once, my people helped the settlers and trusted their promises of friendship. But then Texas got incorporated into the United States, and that meant my people were suddenly unwelcome in our own home.

Three. I'm Lipan Apache.

Mama has been teaching me what that third fact means all my life. No matter where my family travels and who we encounter, I am Lipan.

I was born on Ojibwe land in a winter so bitter, my earliest memory is the feeling of cold. Mama says I showed the loons how to really cry, and sometimes the birds and I screamed at each other, like we were sparring with our voices.

Four years later, my Mama remarried on Celtic land; she held my hand during the airplane trip, my first, and when we landed, we cried together. I cried because I was tired and grumpy. She cried because she felt like a rubber band stretched too tight, since her body was rooted to the land an entire ocean away. That's what she claims, anyway. She was probably tired and grumpy too.

We spent two weeks in Limerick to visit my new grandparents. They fed me buttery cookies and taught me how to weave yellow wildflowers into a necklace. At the end of the visit, my Mama wore her finest traditional regalia, a bright yellow camp dress and a pink shawl with yellow fringe. She draped her neck with the good jewelry, dense strands of seed beads clasped by silver. Mama's bride wore a slim white suit. With a kiss, they were married.

On the flight home, when the turbulence frightened me, I held my new Mom's hand, and she patted my head and promised we'd be safe.

I started school on Sioux land; my family lived between a pig farm to the north and an ocean of corn to the south, the kind of corn that tasted sweet but didn't taste *like corn.* No wonder our rent was cheap — 'cause the smell when the wind blew from the north permeated everything. The scent of manure still makes me nostalgic. It's gross but true. Fortunately, we didn't stay on Sioux land long. My family never stayed anywhere for more than a couple years.

Unfortunately, each new land had its own troubles. Some worse than others.

A boy tried to kiss me on Paiute land, eighth grade. It happened in chess club, thirty minutes of gaming between lunch and fifth period. I joined on my first day in the new school because Mama and I often played together. When you're a stranger trying to fit in, it helps to find something familiar and use it as a life raft. Gives you confidence. At least, that's what I've experienced.

The chessboards were all different because the students had to bring their own. For a couple minutes, I hesitated in the doorway of the classroom and watched the other club members, who seemed happy to ignore me. I saw this brown-haired white boy named Brandon — he was in my morning math class — open a polished wooden case and take out a prehistoric-themed chess set with dinosaur-shaped pieces. Velociraptor pawns, pterodactyl bishops, triceratops knights. The king and queen were both T. rexes, but the king rex wore a crown. The dinos were so cute, they made me smile, so I stepped up to Brandon's table and said, "Hi. Can I play?"

He got all serious and replied, "No." Then, when the smile dropped off my face, Brandon grinned like the Cheshire cat and added, "I'm kidding. Yeah, sure. Sit down."

It took a moment to work up the enthusiasm for a new smile. That kind of joke bothers me; it's a pet peeve, I guess. Maybe 'cause the punch line is based on the premise that it would be weird to turn down a simple request, but it's not actually weird. I'm well acquainted with the word "no." One time, a cheddar-selling woman at an all-local, organic grocery store said "no" when I asked her for a cheese sample. She had a tray of toothpick-skewered orange cubes, but they were for customers only, and I guess the box of maple sugar candy I'd just bought didn't count. Another time, I had to ask four strangers on the school bus, "Can I sit here?" and got three "nos" before somebody moved her backpack from an empty aisle seat and said "yes."

But Brandon was just being friendly, and he had a dinosaur chess set, and I had no allies yet on Paiute land, so I chuckled and said, "You got me," and moved a velociraptor to e4. "My name is Grace."

"Like the virtue?" He said "virtue" in a weird way, almost like the word had a hidden meaning.

"Yep."

It quickly became clear that about half of chess club spent more time on their phones than in the game, but Brandon wasn't part of that half. He timed our moves with a redwood chess clock and only spoke during my turn. Our conversation was therefore full of dramatic pauses, although the spoken content was mundane. Typical nice-to-meet-you stuff.

"Where are you from?" he asked. There are hundreds of Native tribes, bands, and nations in the United States, and by that time, I'd drifted across dozens of their lands. None, however, had been home.

"I moved here from Vermont," I said, remembering the lush green in the northeast. They were pretty in small doses, but after a while, those mountains made me feel like a rat in a maze, imprisoned by the land itself. From my family's rental cabin in Vermont, it was impossible to see the horizon at sunset. The light just winked out behind a western peak every evening. I started to have nightmares about giants, about the world disappearing in their shadows.

"Yeah, but where are you *from*?" Brandon repeated. And I realized it was that kind of question. Where are you *from* from, brown-skinned girl?

"Texas," I said. "I am Lipan Apache from the Little Breech-clout band, Tcha shka-ózhäyê, of the Kuné Tsé. My ancestral lands. I return every year for the Nde Daa Pow Wow."

There was a long silence, but it wasn't Brandon's turn. "Oh," he finally said. "That's interesting."

"Where are you from?" I asked.

"Florida," he said. "I moved here six years ago."

"But where are you *from*?"

He laughed. "Okay. Funny."

"Is it?" I took one of his velociraptors. "Your move."

When the bell rang a couple minutes later, Brandon photographed our game board before he collected the pieces. "Can we continue this next time?" he asked.

"Uh-huh. See you Tuesday."

Actually, the next time we saw each other was ten minutes later, in fifth period, English. Brandon waved me over to the desk beside his. "Do you have your books yet, Grace?" he asked. "You can share mine!"

"I'm all set up," I said. But the offer was still appreciated.

That's how it went for several weeks. We'd sit side by side three classes a day, eat lunch at the same table, and, every Tuesday and Thursday, continue a game of chess that sometimes felt like playing tug-of-war with a clone. Oh, the pieces disappeared one by one, but nobody kept an advantage very long. By week six, just our kings and a few velociraptors remained.

"We can call it a draw," I suggested.

Brandon whipped out a pocket-sized spiral notebook and consulted it. "Actually," he said, "based on time, I win. You spent two-hundred minutes thinking. My time is less than ninety."

"Congratulations," I said. He stuck out a hand, and it took me a moment to recognize the gesture as an offer to shake. The whole ceremony was a bit much, considering that he won on a technicality. But I didn't want to be a sore loser over a board game. That's not a good look. Then again, "insufferable winner" is probably a worse look.

"Okay," I said, laughing. "So official."

"If you want official," he said, "there should be a kiss too."

When our hands clasped, he leaned forward, his eyes shut and his lips pursed. I tried to pull away, but Brandon's grip tightened, so I used my free hand to grab him by the chin, halting his lunge just a few inches from my face. "Stop," I said.

Brandon looked at me with wide eyes; they were a pale shade of brown with the hint of something greenish. I'd never seen them so clearly before, since I rarely make eye contact with anybody. In my family, it's considered rude, not a sign of friendship or trustworthiness. But now, I held his stunned gaze.

"I just . . ." he started. The chess club people around us were staring, their faces a mixture of amusement and fascination. No offense to chess, but Brandon and I were probably providing the most entertainment they'd ever known in that half hour between lunch and fifth period. Only our supervisor, an English teacher with her nose in a paperback book, was oblivious to the drama.

"What?" I asked.

"Jesus. It was just a kiss on the cheek. Sore loser."

"Come on. This isn't about chess."

"Suuuure. Don't make things weird. The US is puritanical. In Europe, everyone kisses each other. It's literally a handshake." Was he speaking loudly because he was angry, or because he was acutely aware of the audience to our conversation?

"For future reference," I said, "none of that matters. Ask next time."

"Uh. Yeah. There won't be a next time."

By his defensive tone, Brandon meant that to be an insult, but I was relieved. No more kisses. Fine. With.

Me. At the time, I didn't realize that he was referring to more than unwanted physical contact. Things between us changed. We still sat side by side in class, but whenever our teacher assigned a group project, Brandon turned his back on my desk and waved at a student across the room. He stopped attending chess club, which left me the odd person out, so I stopped attending too. And at lunch, Brandon moved into the center of his friend group and all but ignored me at the edge of the table.

It took a couple weeks of passive-aggressive Brandon before I got that he wanted nothing to do with me anymore. Had we ever really been friends? I convinced myself that it didn't matter. Some people had spring cleaning; I had summer packing. A chance to throw all my belongings into a few cardboard boxes and leave my personal baggage behind. All I had to do was avoid Brandon until the inevitable move in one or two years.

As luck had it, I didn't need to wait that long. In late April, as the school year entered its final stretch in a flurry of pep rallies and cheer that flowed around me but didn't sweep me up, I returned home to a stack of cardboard boxes in the living room. They smelled like ripe fruit and wine; Mama and Mom must have collected them from the liquor store dumpster and the grocery store downtown. We never bought boxes, and in the long run, that probably saved my parents a thousand dollars. Mama popped up from behind a mound of cardboard. Her hair was bound in a high ponytail, with a bandanna wrapped across her brow.

"What's this?" I asked. "Are you building a fort?"

"Grace," she exclaimed, "we're going home!"

Typically, she faced moves with a somberness appropriate for all the expenses, stress, and unknowns of relocating to a strange new place. But that day? She was beaming. It weirded me out.

"We have a home?" I asked.

"Always. But now we can actually live there."

I must have seemed confused — that's no surprise, since my emotions tend to shape my face like it's clay under a sculptor's hands — because she followed with, "We're going to Texas, and we're *staying*."

"When you say 'staying' . . ."

"I mean it. Buying a house. Starting a garden. Getting a dog. Grace. Grace, do you know what this means?"

I did and I didn't. *Home* had always seemed beyond our reach, like we were knights chasing the Holy Grail. My mama was born near the border, just a few miles away from the birthplace of her mother, grandmother, great-grandmother, great-great-grandmother, great-great-great-grandmother . . . well, you get the point. Since our people didn't have a reservation, though, she had to leave when a flood destroyed her parents' house and they couldn't afford to stay. When Mama spoke of the warmth and beauty of the desert, she always smiled, if only wistfully. Homesickness followed us across every territory like a ghost that haunted my family of three.

But what would it mean to be still? To stop running — not from something but to something — because it wasn't necessary anymore. Would I be disappointed? Bored? Would I feel trapped, like I did every time we lived among mountains?

"It means change, I guess," I said. "But why now? Can we actually afford a house? Did Mom find a job?" Mama always said we'd buy our own place when she'd saved up enough money for my college education, and that was a high bar to meet.

"She hasn't yet," Mama said, "but she will. It's time." For a moment, I thought that was all the answer I'd get. But then she continued, "I've been thinking about the future of our tribe. Sometimes, I wonder . . . if we found a way to be in Texas sooner, would I be on the council now? Maybe. You shouldn't have to wonder the same thing."

"It's not too late for you, Mama."

"You're right. I'm going to throw in my hat for director of education." She tilted her head thoughtfully. "You'd make a good chairwoman someday."

"Noooo. I'm too much of a loner for a leadership role," I said.

"There's nothing wrong with being an introvert." She squeezed my shoulder affectionately. "It's not a popularity contest, anyway. Well. Maybe a little bit. The thing is, a good leader knows our ways and loves our people and is not afraid to fight for them."

"You think that's me?"

"Yes," she said.

I smiled.

"There are boxes in your room," Mama said. "Don't worry about packing yet, though. We can go slow until summer. A couple boxes a day."

"When are we actually leaving?"

She shrugged. "Whenever we're ready."

"Why not tonight, then?" I asked.

She shook her head, amused. "Because somebody needs to finish eighth grade."

"Fine. Guess it's just six weeks." Six weeks of avoiding Brandon and passing classes. Shouldn't be too hard, I figured. I'd just keep doing what I was doing.

Unfortunately, the universe had other plans.

Our math teacher loved group work as much as our English teacher. Both of them claimed it taught important teamwork and communication skills. That may be true. Honestly, it just taught me to envy people with friends. They did group work in easy mode.

Well, after the chess incident, Ms. Welton went, "Pair up. We're doing worksheets today." I turned to the right, but my usual buddy was absent.

Movement caught my eye; from across the room, a hand shot up, and a familiar voice asked, "Can I be in a group of three, Ms. Welton?" That's Brandon for you; he was the kind of student who didn't wait to be acknowledged before speaking, as if the act of hand raising was just a symbolic gesture. When we were friends, I figured he was too excited about learning to wait. But now I think differently. His quirk lost its charm fast.

"Who still needs a buddy?" Ms. Welton asked.

I ignored her question, planning to sneakily complete the group worksheet by myself. It wouldn't be the first time. Maybe that's why my plan fell through: Ms. Welton expected it.

"Grace?" she asked.

"Yes?"

"Do you need a buddy?"

"Need? No . . ."

"Work with Brandon, please." She handed me a single pink worksheet. Great. We had to share.

Screech screech screeeeeech. Brandon's desk made a nails-on-the-chalkboard sound as he scooted it across the tile floor. "I'll do odds," he said, "and you do evens."

"All right."

I placed the assignment between us; it covered the half-inch gap separating our desktops, like a flimsy bridge. The paper made me think about Brandon's chessboard and the slow-motion dinosaur battle that had petered out, unresolved, between us. Was Brandon thinking the same thing? About unsettled games? He had whipped out a piece of lined scratch paper and was speeding through an equation, as if racing to the answer. Good idea; the sooner we finished, the better.

On your mark, I thought. *Get set. Go.*

At first, Brandon and I kept a similar pace. He answered #1 as I answered #2; he answered #3 as I answered #4; but as I answered #6, #8, and #10, Brandon remained stuck on #5. That made me nervous, 'cause we only had one period to do sixteen questions, and I didn't want to be penalized because my *buddy* was too proud or sore or whatever to ask for help. I glanced at question #5, did some calculations, and said, "The answer is C."

He hunched over his scratch paper, as if hiding it from the eyes of cheaters.

"Question five," I said. "The answer is C."

"I'm working on it."

"You don't have to, though. I just told you the answer."

"Okay."

I returned to question #12. About five minutes later, he filled in an answer bubble on our shared worksheet. I shit you not: He thought the answer was B.

"That's not right," I said. "It's C."

"I got B."

"It's a trick question. I'll go through the calculations with you. . . ."

"Just do your work," he said.

"Our *group* work?"

He hunched over his scratch paper, a signal that our conversation — if you could actually call it a conversation — was over. I stared at the wrong answer, which had been penciled in so confidently, it would be difficult to completely erase from the brightly colored sheet.

"Right," I said. "I'm not doing this with you."

When I stood, he finally started to say something, but I didn't have time for Brandon's games. I swiped the worksheet off our desks and made a direct line to Ms. Welton's desk. My so-called "buddy" watched me from his chair, mouth agape, like I'd just slipped into a clown costume and started dancing around the classroom.

"Miz?" I said. "I need another group."

Ms. Welton had an expressive pair of thick black eyebrows; at my request, they shot up behind her red-framed glasses. "Why, Grace?"

"Brandon's ignoring me, and I don't want a low grade 'cause of him."

She shook her head. "I'll talk to —"

"Ms. Welton, can you please just give me my own paper?"

"I understand it's difficult sometimes," she said, "but in the real world, you need to associate with all kinds of people. Find ways to get along and work together. It's important."

Real world? Did she think that everyone younger than eighteen lived in a simulation? I leaned forward and continued in an almost-whisper, afraid I'd start shouting otherwise. "Brandon tried to kiss me, and I said no. Now he's treating me like garbage. I don't have to work with anybody who disrespects me that way. *Ever.*"

I didn't think my math teacher's eyebrows could go any higher, but they managed somehow. Ms. Welton handed me a new pink worksheet. "If you need help finishing on your own," she said, "please let me know."

"Thank you."

After transferring answers from the old to the new assignment, I returned to the island Brandon had made with our desks. "We're working by ourselves now," I said.

"Oh."

He just looked at me for a bit, like he expected more. An explanation? An accusation? An apology? I gave him nothing. About a minute later there was a *screech screech*, and the space between us widened.

During the next group project, Ms. Welton let me join a team of three. My buddies and I finished the assignment ten minutes early and spent the rest of class talking about superheroes in nondisruptive indoor voices. A few days later, when Ms. Welton returned my work, I noticed that she wrote "Great Job!" beside my grade. I folded the neon-pink sheet of paper into a photograph-sized rectangle and tucked it inside my scrapbook of mementos.

It was a reminder of my real ally on Paiute land.

SHIFT

BY JASON REYNOLDS

bottle rocket babies
locked in safes unsafe
buried beneath belittling
eventually explode
fuses aint but so long
besides they were
made to be tectonic
fireworks that scream
and star and spark
into the ether
and the ethos
of the

shovel-handed
who will someday
shake and wobble
their legs will wishbone
as the quo violently splits
and bottle rocket babies
the minors
will be miners
of their own fire
though always
always blamed for a fault
line they had no part
in creating

THE HELPERS

BY L. D. LEWIS

Sasha

9:45 p.m.

Off soon. Pizza tonight?

ALLIE STARED AT HER SISTER'S message a moment before answering. The city had been in the throes of a heat wave for the better part of a week now and not even night was cool enough. The air was still thick, still humid, and breathing felt like drowning. Eating somehow seemed like it made things hotter.

She sent Sasha a noncommittal thumbs-up and crossed the street.

Somewhere to the south, bass rattled center city. The chants of protest crowds bounced off of tall buildings and met the block as distant, warbled echoes. The people who passed her on their way to join the fray seemed more excited than angry tonight. Maybe there was progress. Maybe the heat had everyone a little delirious.

The neighborhood had begun its road to gentrification. The shops still had signs subtitled in Spanish, but as Allie walked the familiar cracked sidewalks to the corner store, she passed row houses that had been given fresh paint jobs and new windows with young white couples to occupy them, their AC units humming as those occupants without mingled, melting on stoops.

A small, light-skinned old woman named Mrs. Harlow sat in her window as she did most nights, with a fan blowing her lace curtains and the scent of the flowers in her window box out toward the street. She had more of a glare about her than a gaze, as if she liked absolutely none of what she saw, but Allie saw her soften whenever she greeted her.

"Doing alright there, girlie?" said Mrs. Harlow as Allie paused in front of her house. She had a deep, gravelly voice, as if she'd sung or smoked for years.

"I think I might burst into flames in a minute here," Allie replied. "You're up late tonight."

"Mm-hmm, so is everybody else. You know me, I gotta know what's going on."

Allie smiled. "I'm making a quick run. Do you need cold water or anything from Mr. Donovan's?"

"You Carmichael girls are always so helpful." She chuckled. "No, baby, my water gets cold enough just fine. You can tell Miss Sasha when she gets in, though, to come see me. I don't think this new medicine my doctor's got me on is doing my blood pressure right."

"I will." Allie nodded. Sasha was the neighborhood medical professional, and she looked after the residents when she could. She was a paramedic. Allie was visiting for the summer and Sasha's shifts were long and often left Allie to entertain herself. That usually meant watching TV and alternating pizza and Chinese takeout.

She crossed another street and turned into the corner store, grateful even for the barely functioning air conditioner inside.

"Hey, young lady," the shop owner called. He sat behind the counter, framed by colorful shelves of all the things people still smoked, his attention on a small TV screen. His gray cat, Gustavo, had positioned himself atop a chip rack between the freezer wall and an oscillating fan.

"Hi, Mr. Donovan," Allie replied on her way to the wall of beverage coolers.

"Yesss . . ." She groaned into the freezer. She closed her eyes as the chill kissed her sweat-soaked skin. She could get away with standing in the open door for maybe thirty seconds before Mr. Donovan snapped his fingers and yelled something about charging her an AC tax.

Twenty-eight seconds in, she grabbed three bottles of water and went to the counter with them. Mr. Donovan reminded her of someone's domino-hustling uncle, all-gray hair slicked back carefully, a thin gold chain peeking from beneath the unbuttoned collar of a coral linen shirt. He shook his head and gesticulated at the screen between bites from a fist of caramel corn.

"Mira. They still at it," he muttered at her.

"This about that man the cops shot?" Allie said, digging money out of her messenger bag.

"Nah, the other thing. Then again, what ain't it about, right?" Mr. Donovan grunted and rang up the waters.

Allie watched as the nightly news recapped the week's protests throughout the city. Early days of clever signs, unified chants, hopeful speeches from the woke and diverse community leaders bled into the collapse of resolve when people started passing out from heat exhaustion around day three. White protesters featured so prominently in daytime coverage somehow disappeared from nighttime footage of tear gas deployment, riot gear, the faces of brown strangers contorted in war cries during clashes with police.

"They got the mayor to step down behind this or that but that ain't what everybody was after," he said, and then raised an eyebrow at her. "Surprised you not out there. All this what kids your age do now, ain't it? Fight that power?"

A pang of guilt shot through Allie's chest. She'd come to the city because it was a place where *things happened* and yet she'd done nothing. There was something intimidating about taking to the streets. It wasn't the danger, exactly. But everyone on the news seemed so sure of themselves and their purpose. She imagined herself being swept up in the throngs into some foreign part of the city too embarrassed to cut the fevered momentum and ask anyone how to get home. She knew she'd stammer live on camera, Jan Wellington from Channel 4 sticking a mic in her face and asking plainly where she stood on the issues of the day, and she'd stare dead-eyed into the lens and belch: "Injustice is bad."

Chyron reads *Area Teen Knows Nothing*.

She cared, though. Injustice mattered. But she was too young to vote, or to count on petitions, and nothing unjust enough had ever happened to her specifically to give her any kind of authority, so who would listen?

The image on the screen shook violently about the same time Allie heard a thundering *BOOM* outside. Jan Wellington all but leapt out of her shot and the camera jolted its focus on a group of protesters fleeing a flash of light and a plume of smoke. Allie caught Mr. Donovan's eye for a brief second before a great warping sound plunged them into darkness.

Before Mr. Donovan could complete his groan, the ground shook beneath them and a sound like a distant transformer popping made Allie jump.

And then there was another. Closer.

The third roared like a freight train rolling up the street. It shattered the shopwindows and sent Allie to the ground covered in glass. The roar grew and continued to shake items from their shelves. Glass bottles fell from open refrigerator doors and smashed against the tile.

Then, all at once, it stopped, and she was left with the sounds of her own panting, her own blood pounding in her ears.

Tires skidded and car alarms sounded. The sky outside was thick with rolling dust when she dared open her eyes. She gingerly brushed small glass shards from her legs and collected herself.

Mr. Donovan came around the counter to help her up.

"You okay?" He coughed.

"Yeah, I think." Allie frowned, reaching for her phone. "What was . . ."

Without another word, both of them peered out of the space where the window had once been at the cloud of gray creeping up the block, and the hole in the skyline where a coffee shop and a dry cleaner's were now sagging brick and mortar into the middle of the street. The road itself rippled and split away from the impact. Neighbors poured out of their homes, each staring agape and silent at the wreck.

Allie felt whole minutes pass, as no one seemed to know what to do.

"I need some help over here!" someone yelled from somewhere in the cloud.

"Eh, it's people in there!" Mr. Donovan yelled in case anyone hadn't heard. He left her side and began milling around with his flashlight.

Sasha.

Panicked, Allie called her sister's phone, but the line rang once and went to voicemail.

"You calling Sasha?" Mr. Donovan asked.

"Went to voicemail," Allie replied. Her voice sounded small and distant to her own ears.

Mr. Donovan stopped his shuffling and eyed her. "She's okay, you know," he said.

Allie nodded but she wasn't sure. Sasha would have at least tried to call her by now.

"Look, you take this and give me your phone." He handed her a flashlight newly packed with batteries he'd just opened and she handed over her phone. "Head home and wait for her but call 911 on your way there, yeah? And when you meet up, call me. My number's in there. We gonna need you."

He handed her phone back and gave her a hard pat on the shoulder before turning back to rummage through his stock.

Allie made her way quickly across the crunching glass into the thick night air. Sirens sounded in the distance. She tried Sasha's phone again and got nothing, so texted her instead:

10:03 p.m.

> I'm fine. Heading home. Where are you?

"Off soon. Pizza tonight?" was still the last message Sasha had sent. Allie chewed a fingernail as she peered out of the living room window at the dark chaos on the street below. Car horns still blared. Cries for help mingled with shouted efforts to organize some relief. People moved in the glow of headlights and bouncing cell phone flashlights through the heavy dust.

Push notifications told her the city had been rocked by a series of explosions, which was perfectly useless information if you lived there. Emergency services were at capacity. "Blackout" was trending on Twitter, which was already flooded with missing persons and videos from every angle. Emergency services sirens could be heard in nearly every Periscope but no one got a shot of the vehicle. She was hoping to spot Sasha's rig. Searching for it had drained her battery down around 30 percent. Her parents' check-in phone calls dropped it down to 15 percent.

Over the din, she heard, "She's bleeding pretty badly."

Panicked at the thought that maybe Sasha had been crushed, she leaned out of the window and pointed a flashlight up the block, stopping where she saw the neighbors crowded onto Mrs. Harlow's stoop. One of them, a man Allie didn't know, squinted in the direction of the light.

"Hey, Sasha up there?" he called.

"No, she's still at . . ." Well, she didn't know where she was. "She's not here."

"You got, like, a first aid kit?" said another man beside him. "Mrs. Harlow's a little banged up."

"Yeah, one sec," Allie replied. She turned the flashlight back into the apartment and scanned for the big yellow street medic backpack she knew Sasha kept in case of emergency. She found it in Sasha's bedroom closet. She checked her phone again for a message from Sasha but there was nothing and her battery was all but dead. Maybe Sasha's phone was destroyed. Maybe she was hurt and couldn't get to it.

Waiting, doing nothing, was no longer an option.

She checked the bag and found a hundred tiny pockets and compartments laden with medical supplies: gloves, gauzes, a dozen types of bandages and bandannas, Sudecon wipes, and various ointments. She grabbed a clutch of pale blue breathing masks from a front pocket and put one on. Whatever that building was made of, it was probably a good idea not to breathe it in.

She dropped some bottles of water into the bag along

with her phone's charger in case she found power somewhere outside, and left a note scrawled in Sharpie on a
pizza menu taped to the door:

PHONE DIED. BE BACK WHEN I FIND YOU.

The dust and debris looked like thick flakes of heavily
falling snow passing through Allie's flashlight beam.
She approached her neighbors, each of them caked with
sweat-streaked dust, and held the light unsteadily on
Mrs. Harlow, who appeared to be bleeding from the
head. The dust had stemmed the stream of blood, leaving a matted, dark patch just along the silver of her
hairline.

"Doorframe was leaning so we had to break it down
to get her out . . ." a burly Black man with a sledgehammer was saying to a woman leaning over Mrs.
Harlow. "Blast must have shifted this whole block."

"Yeah, I couldn't get in my front door just now either.
You check the other houses?" the woman replied. Allie
recognized her as one half of a white couple who lived
next door in the house with the new blue shutters and
tomato garden out front. Mrs. Harlow side-eyed her
more than anyone on a good day and didn't seem
pleased to be in her care just then.

"Nah, we saw her first," said one of the men.

The woman turned to Allie. "You the medic?"

"Me? No. I have a bag of medical supplies, though," Allie replied.

"That you, Allie girl?" said Mrs. Harlow, squinting into the flashlight beam.

"It's me, Mrs. Harlow."

"I'm Claire," the woman introduced herself.

"John," said the older man with the sledgehammer.

"Mack," said the younger one. "We thought maybe she fell or something and —"

"You could ask me, you know. I was there. I could tell you," Mrs. Harlow snapped, and looked pointedly at Allie, as if she was the only one there worth speaking to. "I was leaning out the window when that blast went off and rocked the house. The window shattered around me and I hit my head on the frame ducking back in. It wasn't no brick."

"I apologize, Mrs. Harlow," John said patiently. "Roads are garbage. There's no way to get anyone hurt to the hospital. Firehouse is the next best bet but that thirty-minute walk is an hour now on the back streets with all the obstructions."

"And I only know a couple of *Grey's Anatomy* seasons' worth of first aid," said Claire.

Allie pinched the flashlight between her cheek and shoulder and rummaged through the pockets of the bag for something that might trigger a memory of health class or an episode of *Chicago Fire*; of Sasha talking about a head-injured patient when she came home to visit, her hands flying the way they always did in pantomime of saving a life. A small book glinted at her from a rear compartment. She pulled it out to find the cover wrapped in yellow reflective tape with a red cross at the center. The title page read "Street Medic Handbook."

"Found something," she said, flipping through the worn pages. A dozen acronyms were bolded, circled, highlighted, each a different procedure checklist, and her sister's handwriting was scribbled in the margins. Finally, she went back to the table of contents to find a section on head injuries.

She went down a short checklist. The patient was responsive, hadn't lost consciousness, clearly didn't seem disoriented.

"What kind of wound is it?" Allie asked.

"Mrs. Harlow, I'm going to pour water on this just so we can get a clear look at it, okay?" said Claire.

"Mm-hmm," Mrs. Harlow muttered in her disapproving way. "Whatever gets y'all to stop fussing the fastest."

Claire dribbled water over the wound and dabbed it away from over Mrs. Harlow's eye with the bottom of her shirt. "Doesn't look too bad. Not deep, not open."

Allie read from the book. "'Scalp — external laceration; may look really bloody because there are a lot of capillaries in the scalp; treat like other lacerations, but care should be given to protect vital centers like the brain, spine, et cetera.' Easy enough."

"There's nothing wrong with my spine," Mrs. Harlow groaned.

Allie handed Claire a bundle of bandages and some tape and the two of them got to work cleaning and wrapping the wound.

"You doing okay, girlie?" Mrs. Harlow asked quietly between winces.

"A little freaked out, honestly," Allie replied. "Haven't heard from Sasha since before the explosions. She was on her way home."

"Oh, she's okay." Mrs. Harlow gripped Allie's hand firmly and gave her a serious look. "You don't worry. She's probably out here somewhere helping like you. Got trapped on the other side of that mess."

Allie nodded. She'd been trying not to look at the ruin in the street. She could imagine Sasha somewhere beneath it.

"I haven't heard from my husband either," Claire said, ripping off a section of tape with her teeth. "He was on his way home from the airport. Cell signal's been spotty. I can't get through."

Allie said nothing. She watched as Claire focused on very specific placing of tape along Mrs. Harlow's bandage, the way she firmly but gently pressed it into place, as if a moment's focus on anything else would wreck her. It wasn't enough to say she was sure Mr. Claire's Husband was fine, that he would be home soon just like Sasha. With all the wreckage in the city, it was beginning to dawn on her that not everyone could have survived.

She felt sick.

With Mrs. Harlow patched up, the group had fallen silent and turned to the scene around them. The sky was orange in places where fires were burning in the city. The smoke and dust hung like a curtain. Other strangers were shadows in the street, alternating between rushing to this or that task and standing in clusters to stare in disbelief at the rubble. Across the street, a girl about Allie's age sat on her stoop with her leashed puppy cowering between her legs. She'd started lighting a row of candles beside her, when someone called from a few houses down and told her to put them out in case of a gas leak. So she sat wide-eyed in the dark instead, and stared at the rubble.

"What *happened*?" Claire wondered aloud.

"Gas line, terrorist attack, aliens . . ." John shrugged.

"Yeah, I'm hearing a lot of 'terrorist attack.'" Mack scratched at the scruff on his neck.

"State-approved or the other kind?" said Mrs. Harlow.

"Possible retaliation for getting the mayor to step down?" said Claire.

"Probably someone taking advantage of the chaos. Guarantee we won't know tonight, though," said John.

Allie heard a vibration and got excited that maybe it was her phone, before Claire's lit up in her hand.

"Oh, thank God." Claire gasped and then immediately looked like she wished she hadn't. "It's Charlie. He's still at the airport."

Allie nodded. There were so many things wrong with feeling jealous of Claire.

"Anybody know what time it is?" Allie said, hoisting Sasha's bag onto her back. "We should check the other houses, right? See if there's anyone still trapped?"

"Going on midnight," Claire said.

John and Mack nodded.

"Well, let's go." She needed to stay busy. It meant getting closer to the wreckage, but maybe it would take so long, Sasha would call her.

Maybe.

"I'll stay with Mrs. Harlow. See if I can get in touch with Charlie," said Claire. Mrs. Harlow rolled her eyes.

Allie handed them a couple of blue masks and a bottle of water for want of something more helpful to do. "My sister's name is Sasha. If you see her . . ."

"I know, honey." Mrs. Harlow nodded. "I know."

Allie waited at the bottom of the stairs at each house as John and Mack stopped, knocked, and called out. That's what most of the street was now. The ground was covered in shattered glass from busted windows and crunched beneath Allie's feet as she shifted her weight impatiently. She checked her phone whenever she felt an hour had passed, and tried calling Sasha or waving it around for a signal so she could get any delayed text messages. Just once, she wanted to dial and hear the ringtone nearby. Sasha was obsessed with this song from a vintage *Tom and Jerry* episode. Some country mouse yodeling.

Allie would give anything to hear that stupid song just now.

So far they'd gotten five people and two terrified dogs out of the slanting buildings. They'd borrowed the ladder atop some electrician's van to get an elderly man and his small, ugly-adorable dog from a second-story apartment over a coffee shop and used bookstore. The worst injury between them was a broken arm, which Allie used the handbook to splint, but nothing that needed to be iced was getting iced and nothing that needed stitching was going to be stitched tonight.

The coughing was becoming more prevalent the closer they got to the wreckage. The dust burned her eyes and she wished for goggles to somehow appear in the bag she now knew every inch of. She started handing out masks to bystanders while she waited for Mack and John and whoever else to present her with someone who needed bandaging.

A couple of people in beige-blend military uniforms plucked at slabs of concrete from the pile of collapsed building, pausing intermittently to yell, "Trapped, call out!" Allie waited with them, listening hard for sounds that weren't the ringing or smothered vibrating of buried cell phones. She wasn't sure if she wanted to hear Sasha's voice. The thought made it even harder to breathe.

No one called out.

They went back to digging.

"You're not getting in here!"

Allie's attention snapped back to a house with an orange door before her, where John and Mack were trying to coax someone out through the window.

"Sir, we're here to hel —" Mack tried.

"What y'all come to fix with sledgehammers? This ain't *The Purge*!" an incredulous voice scoffed from inside. "I will not be looted today — no, sirs!"

The men exchanged confused, frustrated expressions. "We just want to get you looked at and see if you need any medical attention, that's all," said John.

"Sasha Carmichael out there?" said the voice.

They turned to look at Allie, who gulped and trudged her way up the stairs.

"No," she called. "I'm her sister, though. My name is Allie."

"Well, Allie, my name is Mr. Curtis Brown. Do you know these men?" the voice said loudly.

She thought a moment. Until a couple of hours ago, no she didn't know them. She didn't much know them now. They could have once been people who robbed houses using sledgehammers but it hadn't occurred to her. She did feel confident enough to say now, though, that they weren't going to Purge this man.

"Yes, we've been going door-to-door to get people out. Sometimes we patch them up. See? I have Sasha's manual and everything." She thrust the little reflective book in front of the window, bracing for him to shoot at it with a gun it hadn't occurred to her a moment earlier he might have. She snatched the book back quickly.

Mr. Brown didn't say anything.

"Even if you're not hurt, Mr. Brown, we still want you to come outside," Allie tried. "The buildings aren't safe on this block. The blast knocked a bunch of stuff loose and we don't want it to crush anybody."

There was nothing now. No response from inside for full seconds. The three of them stood on the porch and looked at each other before Allie swallowed the knot in her throat and leaned across the broad bannister to peer into the window with her flashlight.

"Mr. Brown, it's Allie, I just want to look at you. If you're okay, we'll leave you alone."

The light traveled across the room, visibility obscured by the increasing presence of dust. Items had been tossed from shelves and tabletops and some of the floor was strewn with the things that had broken. Mr. Brown — if this was him — was a thin brown middle-aged man seated dazed on the floor in the far corner with blood glazing his palms.

"Mr. Brown, are you bleeding?" she asked him.

"Yeah," he replied. "Glass is all in 'em."

His speech seemed tired, forced. He blinked hard and his eyes listed over in her direction. Something was wrong. Allie felt panic rising in her chest. He could be concussed. He could die and she was the only thing resembling medical help for blocks.

"Can you come to the window? The guys will pull you out and we can look at you," she tried.

Mr. Brown shook his head and appeared to drift off to sleep.

She turned to Mack and John. "You have to get him out of there now. I'd go in but I can't carry him back out."

Mack tested the door to see if it would budge without greater violence, but John ended up having to slam the hammer into its locks repeatedly. When he forced the door open, a groaning, splintering sound rang out and seemed to resonate down the block. Strangers with assumed authority shouted "Stand back!" and "Move!" behind them. Allie held her breath and covered her ears, waiting to scream forever as the row homes went down like dominoes, with Mr. Brown being crushed first.

But nothing collapsed. The ground barely shook. John and Mack decided with a look to rush in and grab Mr. Brown and rush back out. They carried him out between them and placed him on the sidewalk, where Allie took a long time examining him to figure out what she needed to look up in the manual.

His hands were badly cut, with nauseatingly large slivers of glass embedded in both of them. That was the easy part. His pupils were also slow to respond to her flashlight, and while he could hear and communicate, he was bleeding from both his ears. Far as she knew, she only had the resources to help his hands.

She gave him some water and cleaned his hands, removing only what she thought might not make him bleed too much. She wasn't sure how much he had to spare and didn't want him going into shock. She wrapped his hands as best she could and propped him against a large flowerpot that was mostly just dirt.

Her head was beginning to ache as she looked around. It was still so dark, so hot, and hard to breathe. She rinsed dust from her eyes with now-warm water and blotted at it with the inside of her shirt while she checked her phone. No signal. No new messages. It was after one. She turned it off again and began to pace. Her heart pounded.

What am I doing?

"I don't know what to do," she told John and Mack. "I don't know how to help him. He has a concussion or something. The handbook thing says to stabilize him and get him to the hospital but we can't do that."

I don't know what to do, she thought. *I don't know why this happened. I don't know where Sasha is. I don't know what to do if she's . . .*

Allie put her hands to her knees and gulped air to sate the sensation that she was drowning in all the things she didn't know.

"Look," said John, his voice calm behind the mask. "How about we take a break?"

"How can we take a break? Look at this!" she shrieked. Her eyes burned again but it was their attempt at conjuring tears. Her body felt too parched to cry them. "There are people in there! How do you take a break when there are people in there?"

"Kid, I get it. But this shit is a lot. If you need a break, you take it," John insisted.

"How about this . . ." said Mack. "We get these last two doors, then we take Mr. Brown up by Mrs. Harlow's with the others, see what the roads are looking like or ask around about medical checkpoints. Take fifteen minutes to regroup a little bit away from the dust."

Allie hesitated but nodded. They were done with this side of the block now anyway. Fifteen minutes to decide what to do next wasn't unreasonable. She picked up the bag and stared up the street while she waited beside Mr. Brown for the men to knock on the last two doors. Things were brighter this way, with all the headlights, all the flashlights pointed at the rubble behind her. Maybe she would stop back by the apartment to flush out her eyes properly and see if Sasha had checked in.

Glass broke across the street and Allie jumped. Two men in a shouting match were jostling each other against a brick wall.

"I know you did this!" A young brown man pointed aggressively at an equally young white man who was quickly losing ground despite the smugness on his face.

"I said don't fucking touch me!" the white guy yelped. His chin was stuck out in what Allie's daddy called the "I can't fight" position.

"Come on, cut this shit out," said one of the military men. He and a few others stepped between the two arguing men and began to push them apart.

"Nah, his people came out here and blew all this shit up trying to Make America Great," said the brown guy. And when his target began frothing at the mouth again, he got louder. "I know it was you! I know it was you 'cause *as usual* don't nobody in the neighborhoods that got hit look like y'all."

"See, this is why nobody takes you people seriously," said the white man, smiling more now and feeling safer.

A collective, incredulous *"You people?"* swept the crowd. "You'll do anything for attention. Starting fights with strangers and probably blowing your own sh —"

"Whoa!" the crowd roared, and some of the men who'd broken it up began to turn on him.

Beneath the din of violent chaos rumbling in front of her, she thought she heard a tapping noise somewhere in the rubble behind her.

"Shhh! Shut up! I can't hear!" Allie yelled, and the collective turned to her. "Neither one of you knows anything, alright? Y'all hated each other yesterday and you're both in the dark, and you stink, and you're scared, and you're pissed off like everyone else today. *Shut up.*"

She turned and took careful steps toward the concrete heap and hissed a violent "shh!" as the neighbors began to mutter again.

The group went silent.

There it was. A staccato, metallic rapping on rebar or exposed pipes echoing from somewhere within the pile.

"Call out!" Allie yelled as helpers began to mill about again.

The cry was indistinct — a woman's muffled scream of one, two syllables at best — but Allie heard it and sprang onto the rubble before she could convince herself it was Sasha.

"Red rocks! Red rocks!" someone called behind her. "The red is where it's safe to step."

Allie looked down at where flashlight beams bounced off of slabs of concrete spray-painted with red Xs, forming a somewhat-less-treacherous path along the top layer of rubble.

"Help! Somebody help me!" her voice squeaked out as she dropped her bag and began hurling the largest pieces of concrete she could lift from the area where she heard the banging. The neighbors arranged themselves around her to lift debris from the place she indicated in her frantic tossing.

Soon, her chest burned and she was finding nothing but more wreckage, when one of the military guys shouted, "I got someone!" a few yards to Allie's right. She made her way over to him carefully, and saw that he was clasping a dusty, bruised, and scraped hand poking up out of the debris. Allie didn't recognize the hand.

"Can you tell me your name?"

"Mercedes Reyes," said a woman's desperate voice. "My leg is broken."

Allie's heart sank so fast she thought she'd topple off the pile.

"Mercedes, my name is Mike. I'm a United States Marine. We're going to get you out of there." He turned to Allie. "You good?"

Allie swallowed hard. This wasn't Sasha. She could be so close; three feet in any direction if anyone cared, if anyone would bother to look. Or she could be nowhere. Anywhere.

But Mercedes was right here. And Mercedes needed her.

Allie nodded.

"Okay. I need you to hold her hand. Keep her talking if you can. If she's in distress, if her grip goes slack, you let me know. We'll move as fast as we can."

Allie stretched out and lay prone atop the rubble, then took Mercedes's hand and held it tightly. She couldn't see Mercedes's face, just bare inches of her arm.

"Mercedes, my name is Allie," she said in as high spirits as she could muster. "I'm going to stay here with you while Mike digs you out."

By the time she looked up again, everyone who had been standing idle was deconstructing the pile, moving the stones to neat rows along the sidewalks. Mr. Curtis, who was still sitting where they'd left him, had his phone out and was presumably calling Sasha's phone, too.

Allie didn't know what time it was. The night had already gone on forever. And while she made small talk with Mercedes as the neighbors dug her out, she thought about Sasha. How she loved this work, how she'd moved here to do it. How she only liked that ridiculous ring-tone because Allie hated it. How they should have been arguing over pizza places tonight.

When they pulled Mercedes free, Allie knew enough to splint the broken leg and give her water, tend to any of the small injuries she could. The girl with the dog brought out blankets in case anyone was in shock. It was something she'd seen on TV. She watched as people continued to dismantle the ruins. There was fatigue in everyone's movements now, as if the one rescue was enough. No one moved quickly or with any kind of hope.

The plan was still to move whomever needed the medical attention to the top of the street, where maybe emergency vehicles could see them. Allie started to collect the bag, when she thought she heard the faintest twinkling notes of a country mouse yodeling in the rubble behind her.

She let the others gather the injured, and instead made her way back to the debris in a daze. It was entirely possible that she was emotionally, physically exhausted, and that she was hearing things. But flashing lights glinted off of windows and brick facades overhead. From where Allie was standing, they colored the smoky sky. Somewhere in the handbook, the colors of emergency lights had been mentioned. She idly flicked through the pages in her mind to see if she could remember what it was as she climbed the red path up the mound again.

The other side was a blinding barrage of blue and red and yellow lights. Someone in a truck bed with a megaphone a block away was giving orders Allie only caught the echoes of. Emergency workers distributed supplies from the bed of another truck, and a line was forming near an ambulance.

And Sasha's ringtone whistled beneath it all.

She watched as a group of silhouettes dispersed from a meeting over the front end of a truck. One of them stepped close enough for her to see them answer a phone and shout something into it.

And the ringtone had stopped.

"Sasha?" Allie croaked. It came out quietly, as if she was asking herself.

Quickly, she dug her phone from her pocket and turned it on.

Two bars. Three percent battery.

She dialed Sasha's number for the thousandth time tonight, threw up a quick prayer for whoever may have been listening and held her breath.

The silhouette in the street reached for their phone in time with the ringing on Allie's end. And when they put it to their ear, Sasha's voice came in over the line.

"Allie?"

Allie's skin prickled.

"Sasha!" Allie shrieked, and nearly tossed her phone in the scramble to get down the other side. She mis-stepped a couple of times and slid down loose patches of brick and glass but never took her eyes from her sister, battered, disheveled, gorgeous, and aglow in emergency truck headlights.

Sasha jogged to meet her at the bottom. Allie's body had been weary, heavier than it had ever been until that moment when it sprang her forward into Sasha's arms and hugged her until she felt real.

"I knew you were okay," Sasha sobbed into Allie's shoulder.

"I knew you were, too," Allie sputtered. "Where were you?"

"I got held up. The roads are a mess and folks who couldn't get to the hospital came to the firehouse instead. Took me hours to get this far. Haven't lost anybody yet, though," Sasha said. Allie let her sister inspect her, her hands flying here and there again to see if any harm was hidden from her.

"We have to find a way to tell Mom and Daddy you're okay. Do you know how any of this happened?" Allie asked her.

"No. And it doesn't matter right now. You take care of your people first and let somebody else work on why," said Sasha, exhaling a long, relieved breath at not having found anything missing on her.

Allie nodded. Honestly, she'd been less interested in the why of it anyway while people needed her. She looked around at the scene on this side of the street.

The rubble pile was beginning to be deconstructed as two neat rows of large slabs. Here and there, cell phones were beginning to ring and announce missed notifications. People answered them loudly and tearfully.

"Everybody okay on our side? Mrs. Harlow?" Sasha asked.

"Mrs. Harlow hit her head."

"Better get over there," she said, then whistled to a couple members of her team back by the truck. "Bring the gear; we're going over."

"Well, I left your emergency bag over there, too."

"My what?"

"The bag in the closet with the handbook. We patched Mrs. Harlow up and according to, like, eight different checklists, she seems okay."

"Yeah?" Sasha smirked her intrigue. "Let's see how good a job you did."

Allie led her sister and two other medics up a path of red Xs and down the other side. Mr. Donovan had appeared and was distributing lights, batteries, and water. Progress on moving the injured seemed halted, though, when cell service returned, and neighbors cried relief to loved ones over their phones.

She introduced Sasha to Mike and the others, and then to the people she'd treated as patients, still sitting on the curb.

"This is Mr. Brown and Mercedes. Mr. Brown I think has a concussion and some bad glass damage to his hands. Mercedes we dug out. Her leg's broken and I'm bad at splints, so . . ."

"You splinted her?" Sasha raised an eyebrow.

"Yeah, a few other people up the street, too," said Allie. The night's anxiety seemed to catch up to her suddenly as she looked at the people she'd helped. The world tilted a bit and she felt sick. She hadn't cried once but the threat of it was imminent. How had she done any of this as terrified as she'd been all night?

"I didn't know what else to do," she said, her voice shaking as the tears started to fall. "I was so scared you were . . . that something happened and I just knew I had to keep doing stuff or thinking about you being dead would make it real."

She choked a sob and Sasha hugged her again until she caught her breath. "Hey. *Hey.* Allie, you saved these people's lives. Anything could have happened tonight and they could have died alone in the dark, terrified and waiting for us. Everything you did, even if you just did it because you were scared, was good. It counts. And I'm proud of you."

Allie pulled back and inwardly demanded she get herself together. She blew a tense breath through trembling lips and wiped away her tears, leaving wide, damp streaks in her dust-caked face.

"Okay," she said.

"You good?" Sasha asked after giving her a moment.

"Good." Sasha held out the emergency bag and Allie took it from her, ready for whatever was next.

"I guess we're all lucky you could never stay out of my stuff." Sasha laughed.

FIGHTING THE BLUES

ART BY CONNIE SUN

TAKE A
BREATH.

REMEMBER
YOUR
STORY
MATTERS.

AND
YOU ARE
NOT ALONE.

ARE YOU THE GOOD KIND OF MUSLIM?

BY SAMIRA AHMED

Are you the good kind of Muslim?

The thin-lipped, wrinkled-from-too-much-
   sun neighbor asks
   when your parents are far enough away—
   an absence that gives courage to cowards.

They scowl at you from their top step,
     screen door ajar.
     You stare
     distracted by the unnatural
     jaundice-tinged tan on their arms and neck
     how curious their goal to
     "get some color" when
     your own brown skin inspires their
     sour-milk face.
          Your sun-kissed, impossible-to-replicate
          shade of brown that rests on the edge of
          the curtain of night as it softly descends
          on a summer's eve.

They wait, believing their question deserves an
     answer.
     You pause,
     wide-eyed
     uncertain
     a little confused
     because you are seven years old and no adult
     has ever asked you that before.
     You put your head down and step away,
     words sticking,
     a dry bone lodged in your throat.

When you step away, uneven pavement catches
  your new Mary Janes,
  you trip
  you fall
  you scrape your knee
  crimson bubbles popping up against raw
    pink skin.
  You cry
  your brand-new shiny patent shoes are
    scuffed.
  You hear the screen door slam.

Are you the good kind of Muslim?
  Or the kind that blows stuff up?
  The cashier is young, dirty-blond hair pulled
    into a severe ponytail
  cheeks red and puffed with a hint of baby fat.
  Cruel words and suspicious
  watery-blue eye always
  trigger-finger-ready.
  Is it your name? you wonder.
  Everyone in this small town knows your name
  foreign
  exotic
  impossible to pronounce.

Is that why she scoffs?
Even when her own nameplate is crowded
    with too many syllables,
    and consonants that bang, crash into each
    other?

The oval lacquer jewelry box in your hand looks
    small.
    A delicate Fabergé egg you cup in your curved
        palms. A jewel.
    Pale orange flowers and dark green leaves
        swirling across the smooth vanilla lid,
    waiting for your treasures,
    an unpolished amethyst
    a cloudy rose quartz
    a silver-filigreed hand of Fatima to ward the
        evil away.

You thought you would be ready.
    Older now. Twelve.
    So much wiser than seven.
    Steeled
    experienced
    optimistic.
    You fish for the words that swim around in
        your belly,
        but blood fills your mouth.

Your tongue slashed by shrapnel you thought
  you could swallow.
It is your birthday.
And you wanted to buy yourself a present —
  something beautiful to bring you joy.
You feel the weight of your babysitting money
  in your purse.
It is enough.
You have enough.
You are enough.
You abandon your gift on the counter.
Enough is a word without meaning.

Are you the good kind of Muslim?
  This time, the man asking is brown, like you,
  a trill easily coming to his lips;
  compliant knees bending effortlessly to bus-stop
  squat.
  Not like you,
  he's protected by a glass wall,
  and a badge. And a gun.
  At the airport, he is the Border. He is the Law.
  And he can send you to secondary screening.
      For any reason. For no reason.
      To be questioned.
      To be searched.
      To be handcuffed to the wall.

You've been traveling. You are tired.
    You grit your teeth. You smile.
    You use the right idioms — the ones only an
    American would know.
    You wear the mask, even while it burns.
You want to go home. Even when Home doesn't
    always want you.

Are you the good kind of Muslim?
    Or are you the kind that hates us?
    That we need to ban?
    We can't allow you to infest our great nation.
    I have Muslim friends, you know, wonderful
    people, but there's a cross-section of you
    that have tremendous animosity.
    You understand. This is how you show
    strength.
    The question doesn't surprise you.
    Not from the orange-faced man on TV
        debating your right to exist.
    Not from anyone, really.
    Not this time.

Are you the good kind of Muslim?
    Some questions are daggers,
    forged by guile
    wrapped in a flag

edged with flame.
That pierced your skin so many times,
the scabs formed an armor.
It is heavy.
But you stand
square your shoulders,
challenging them to try and cut you, one
more time.

Are you the good kind of Muslim?
I hold this truth to be self-evident:
I do not answer to you.

AURORA RISING

BY YAMILE SAIED
MÉNDEZ

I DIDN'T EVEN WANT TO COME to the pool, but I couldn't say no to Sadie. Not if I wanted to stay friends with her. I'd known her half my life, since we were eight, but we'd only become close last year. I knew how to read her face and moods, which changed quicker than end-of-summer Utah weather. Right now, her smile was all golden sunshine. The lifeguard was switching, and she'd gotten what she'd been waiting for. *Who* she'd been waiting for.

Clara, Sadie's other friend, had this electric vibe about her that made my skin prickle. She swam around the edge of the pool without making any ripples, a mesmerizing eel hunting for prey.

I shouldn't have let my guard down.

When Sadie's eyes flitted to the boy on the platform and then to me, the smile had turned sharp and cold. She jumped on top of me and pushed my head down. An extra pair of arms pressed hard on my sunburned shoulders before I could lock my knees.

Underwater, I didn't need to fake smile. I clamped my lips so I wouldn't give in and take a big gulp of public pool water. Among us, I could hold my breath the longest, but it's not like I was the Little Mermaid or anything.

Although the water distorted their voices, I heard Sadie command, "Grab her foot! On that side, Clara. Quickly!"

Peeking through chlorine-singed eyes, I braced myself. When Clara's thin fingers took ahold of my foot and tickled me, I was ready. I kicked her hard and wiggled my body with all my strength until the pressure on my head was gone.

"Rory, you kicked my jaw!" Clara cried out.

Not that I cared.

After a quick pat-down to make sure my bikini still covered all the crucial spots, I planted my feet on the pool's floor and jumped up. The sunshine warmed my face, but my lungs weren't ready for the deep breath I took. In my defense, with the many wildfires burning through the Wasatch Front, the air was smoky. I coughed, trying not to think of the faces I was making. I tasted ash on my tongue, and before I knew what I was doing, I spat in the water.

"You're so gross!" Clara complained in a whiny voice.

Sadie laughed. At least she wasn't siding with Clara.

My eyes felt swollen and tender when I rubbed them. Everything — the people in the pool (a couple of chubby blond babies and their young moms not much older than me and my friends), the lounge chairs with rumpled beige towels on them, the wilting trees behind the wrought-iron fence, Mount Timpanogos in the distance — was haloed in an otherworldly red haze. A boy laughed, and when I turned around to see if he was laughing at me, I caught a glimpse of the sun, a bright orange orb, sinking behind the mansions off the golf course. The haze turned the world into a real-life Juno-filtered Instagram post.

The boy's name was Fernando Palacio. Nano.

His deep brown skin glowed with the sunset reflecting off his *Baywatch*-style tank. He raked his fingers through his curly black hair and winked at me. Warmth spread from my belly to the tips of my fingers and toes, all of which were thankfully hidden underwater. I could blame my blushing cheeks on the eerie lighting.

Meanwhile, Sadie posed, sprawled on the pool stairs as if she were on the cover of *Sports Illustrated*'s swimsuit edition. Usually she didn't need to do anything drastic to call a boy's attention, but Nano was different. He never showed any special interest in her. He was a challenge Sadie couldn't resist.

In the back of my mind, a filter-less voice said that he was probably the only reason Sadie had invited me along today. Could it really be a coincidence that Nano was working at the pool the one day this summer we decided to grace it with our presence?

No. With Sadie, there were no coincidences. I'd known Nano since we were babies, although we hadn't been friends in a long time now. Our moms were both from Argentina. A few years ago, though, the friendship fizzled out and died.

All summer long, I'd told Sadie that Nano and I weren't even close anymore, but she either didn't believe me or she was more optimistic than I gave her credit for. And I already thought she was the most positive person in the world. There was nothing Sadie couldn't do.

Last year, she'd made the cheer team after auditions were over. She'd been in Guatemala with her family, working at an orphanage, and Coach Jensen couldn't say no to a special request by Sadie's dad, THE Linden Merrill, CEO and president of Andromeda Steel. Coach Jensen had no problem telling me having my appendix removed in an emergency surgery wasn't a strong enough excuse, though. But then, my last name was Walker, not Merrill, and those were the rules of the game, as my dad said. He didn't say that the only way to play the game was to be *in*. But he didn't need to. I understood it in my soul.

Being Sadie's friend made my life easier, in a way.

I swam toward Sadie while Clara, still rubbing her jaw, got out of the pool and sat on a lounge chair to browse her phone.

"Why didn't you tell me you wanted to see him?" I asked Sadie when I reached her. I really wanted to ask her why she was being a butt, but this wasn't the moment. A breeze blew from the canyon, and goose bumps exploded on my skin. I brushed my hand over my already frizzing hair.

"I had no idea he was here, Rory," she said. Droplets hung on her impossibly long eyelashes. Her gaze flickered to Nano every few seconds.

"You did, and then you drowned me so Nano would look at you," I said, pushing against her shoulder with mine. Side by side, our skin color was the same, bronze, including the myriad freckles that covered our arms and back. I never minded them until Sadie said she hated freckles.

"I didn't drown you." She looked at me with her hurt-puppy expression. "Why are you so extra?"

There was an awkward silence, and then she sighed and slapped her hand on the water, splashing me and making me shiver. "You're supposed to be my best friend. Besides, you almost killed poor Clara." She pressed her lips as if trying to suppress a smile.

It's not like I had no other friends. But Sadie was . . . how shall I put it? She was special.

She wiped her eyes and asked, "Why won't he look at me?" Her voice was choky, frustrated, and I glanced at Nano to contradict her. No one wouldn't look at Sadie, especially not when she wore her white bikini that covered all it was supposed to cover, but that left nothing for the imagination.

But Nano wasn't looking at us. Instead, he chatted with one of the young moms. Her baby splashed as she held him, and she and Nano laughed.

"What are they saying?" Sadie asked urgently. "I think they're speaking Spanish."

"Wait a sec," I said, glad to use my rudimentary language skills, and winked at her.

My swimming form wasn't Olympic perfect, but it wasn't too bad either. In what I hoped was a cool move, I swam across the pool to get a hint of what was keeping Nano's attention from Sadie.

When I reached the other edge, I caught the end of the conversation. They *were* speaking Spanish. He had the same accent as my mom's, but the girl was undoubtedly an American, although her accent was . . . Colombian?

I tried to remember what other Colombians I knew, but the only name that came to mind was Sofía Vergara. My mom detested her show. One summer, my sister, Marina, and I had watched it to spite her, and then Marina had agreed with Mami. But I thought that if Sofía played along with the stereotype and made money, then more power to her.

Nano was saying, "Only five-hundred dollars to go." When he brushed his hair back, I noticed the thin braided rainbow bracelet on his left wrist.

"Sign him up for Saturday, then," the woman said, motioning to her splashing toddler with her head. "I'd love to help out."

"Thanks," Nano said.

Clara was gathering her stuff and shoving it in her striped bag. Sadie ignored her.

Instead, she smiled at me and wiggled her eyebrows, wanting me to get back and tell her everything. I lingered by the edge until the woman and her son got out of the pool. She had a dark red tan line. Her back was going to hurt tonight.

"¿Cómo estás, Aurora?" a voice asked, making me jump. I hadn't noticed Nano slide down into the pool.

Besides the two of us, it was now empty. Nobody else but my family said my name like Nano did, not even me. I couldn't pronounce the soft *r*'s.

He lowered his body until the water covered his shoulders. I stood frozen, feeling Sadie's gaze lasering my back. If I swam away now, I'd lose the chance to introduce them to each other. But if I stayed, I'd have to talk with him, and we hadn't spoken in forever.

Nano swam toward me, and then I had no choice but to wait for him. When he reached me and stood, his hair dripped water on his super-tanned shoulders. He too had freckles but his were almost invisible on his dark skin.

"What?" he asked, a lopsided smile marking the dimple on his right cheek. "Don't you remember me?" he said in Spanish. "We used to nap in the same stroller together, remember? My mom still has the photo on the mantelpiece."

Words crowded at the tip of my tongue. A rush of memories went over me like a wave. S'mores and empanadas in the canyon. Nano's dad running alongside me as I rode my bike. Our moms singing a Ricky Martin song in Spanish. Nano and I stealing Popsicles from the fridge and eating them inside the doghouse. My dog, Coco, had died in his sleep when I was ten years old, and I'd cried bitterly because Nano hadn't had a chance to say goodbye. I hadn't thought of Coco in years, and now the memory of his woolly yellow fur, the ripe scent inside the wooden house. . . . Nano's brother, Ale, finding us and laughing so much he cried.

The feelings couldn't be translated into words. At least not in English, and the Spanish from those childhood days had vanished long ago. That little girl seemed like a stranger.

Nano must have thought the same thing. The light flickered in his eyes, and he looked disappointed, like calling someone in the street and when they turn, you realize you were mistaken.

"I remember," I said in English, and then, I added, "Hola," which came out with the worst gringo accent in the history of forever.

Nano didn't laugh. He just said, "Hola," and when he said it, it sounded natural, like he still spoke Spanish all the time, like I used to when I was his friend.

Suddenly remembering Sadie behind me, I turned to wave her over. "I'm here with my friend Sadie. You know her, right?" I cringed at the sound of my own voice.

Nano waved at her.

Picking up on the cue, she jumped into the water and swam to us. She hugged me, but her eyes were on Nano and Nano alone. "I've seen you around!" she exclaimed, in her charming voice. "You're Fernando?"

When she said his name, it sounded just like me, like a

total gringa. At least she had the excuse of never having been fluent in Spanish. I had no excuse whatsoever.

"Sadie?" he asked.

She smiled her supernova smile. "The one and only."

Nano's smile didn't flicker, but I could feel him rolling his eyes inside. "I've seen you in school." Nano's English had no trace of Spanish, and I envied how he switched from one language to the other so effortlessly. Nano pushed his hair back from his eyes, and without really wanting to, I did the same with mine. By now, my hair had gone full frizz ball, huge, and I pulled it back into an improvised bun and tied it with the emergency elastic I kept on my wrist. All my work flat-ironing my hair for nothing. If only my mom would let me get a Brazilian blowout to get rid of my curls, but she wouldn't budge.

There was no frizz at all on Sadie's hair. But then, she was careful not to get it wet in the pool.

"Let's go, Sadie!" Clara called. "Your mom just texted you!" She held Sadie's phone in her hand and waved it around like a beacon.

Sadie's shoulders tensed. Clara had ruined the moment. But when she turned around, she still smiled at Nano. "See you around," she said, and then, as if she had just remembered, she added, "I'll see you at the junior-class Timp climb, right?"

There was a moment of doubt in Nano's face, and I said, "The climb up to Timpanogos."

Our families had climbed to the top one summer, the last one our families had hung out. He nodded as if the same memory was flashing through his mind.

"I'll see you then," he said to Sadie.

She got out of the pool, throwing a last bewitching gaze at him over her shoulder.

"I hope I'll see you later, Aurora. Say hi to your parents and Marina for me."

"Say hi to your family too."

The ghost of our families' shared history solidified between us. A cloud passed over Nano's eyes, but his smile didn't drop. "I will," he said, and then he got out of the pool and joined the other workers, who were stacking the chairs and tying up the umbrellas for the night.

I watched him for a second too long, regretting the words I didn't say. Trying to remember if I'd ever said sorry about our lives drifting away. In my defense, I'd been only eight when the adults in our families had ruined the friendship.

When I reached Sadie and Clara, I grabbed my pink towel from the floor. I had draped it over the chair, I remembered it clearly, but maybe the breeze had blown it away. Still, I wiped my face with it and put on my cover-up.

"I hate the way they look at us," Clara said, her voice all daggers and glass.

I looked up to see who she was talking about. A man about my dad's age helped Nano with a stubborn umbrella that wouldn't budge.

"You mean them?" I asked, pointing with my chin.

Clara's blue eyes were watery and bloodshot. "They're disgusting. Looking at us like we're pieces of ass, like we don't have feelings. I want to tell the manager or something. In this society, there's no more room for sexual harassment."

Nano and the guy were just working. My frustration at not being able to speak Spanish with Nano, and the rush of memories and unresolved conflicting emotions I was feeling, made me want to throw out a sarcastic or disapproving retort. Clara was pale like a piece of white bread floating in water that not even the ducks would want to eat. And if they looked at us, wasn't it because Sadie had made sure they did?

Clara must have sensed something was brewing and maybe spewing because she clutched her backpack like a shield against her heart.

But Sadie put a hand on my arm and said, "My mom's here. Let's go."

Clara headed to the black Cadillac idling in the parking lot. I followed Sadie, and got into the freezing-cold car.

Before driving away from the country club, Tasha, Sadie's mom, put her sunglasses on top of her head and looked at us through the rearview mirror. "You all look so sun-kissed! Even you, Rory!"

"Especially Rory!" Clara said. I wished she wouldn't talk to me right now. The anger from a minute ago hadn't fizzled out all the way.

The air conditioner was bliss on my burned face.

"You girls should remind each other to wear sunscreen all the time!" Tasha said in a singsongy voice. "Otherwise, you'll end up like me!"

Tasha didn't look that old in my opinion, but she was always fishing for compliments. She wore an impeccably white dress, and her brown hair was pulled back in a tight ponytail.

"We'll get Botox," Sadie said, and Clara laughed.

Sadie turned almost imperceptibly in my direction, and I quickly fake laughed with them.

Tasha's smile was too wide to be genuine. "You two will need Botox for sure, but not Rory, with her beautiful Spanish skin."

There was another silence, and I smiled, like it was expected when someone gave a compliment. Still, my ears started ringing. I hated when the conversation veered to my ethnicity, or race, or whatever.

"Mom!" Sadie complained a second too late. "That's kind of a racist thing to say."

My face was throbbing with heat, and I wasn't sure it was only because of the sunburn. I met Tasha's anxious, frantic eyes on the rearview mirror as she said, "It's not racist, is it, Rory? I meant it with the best intentions! When we were in Guatemala, I was always telling the natives that I envied their skin color. So, so beautiful!"

I smiled back at her, used to playing this game. If I went along, the conversation would change to something else. This wasn't my first rodeo. I just had to get through it. "I'm not offended at all."

Sadie flashed me an apologetic smile.

"I'm glad you're not, baby girl," Tasha said. "Nowadays it's so hard to speak one's mind without being called out. Everything's racist! It's exhausting."

She had no idea.

There was a heavy silence in the car when no one replied, but maybe the others were just wiped out from being at the pool all day.

Out the window, the trees were a blur as we approached Sadie's neighborhood. *Clean Up America* signs from the last local elections dotted most of the lawns. The sight of them intensified my discomfort. I checked my phone. Seeing Nano had made me homesick for my mom, for who she was when I was little. Miraculously, there were no messages from her. Usually she was texting me every five minutes to see if I was still alive. I guess that was one of the hazards of being the youngest of four, her last baby. I typed a quick message to her anyway.

Heading to Sadie's. I saw Nano. He said hi.

I looked at it, and then reconsidered and deleted the last two sentences before pressing send. When she found out about Nano, she'd call me, and then I'd have to answer in the car, having everyone hanging on my every word. I wasn't in the mood for that.

I'd tell her tomorrow when I went back home.

Tasha sang along to the Taylor Swift song playing on the radio. My phone vibrated in my hand.

I looked down at my mom's message.

Okay. When will you be home?

I waited until we'd arrived at Sadie's luxurious house for our sleepover to type a reply.

Tomorrow before noon. Te quiero. Cuidate.

She said, *Bye. Love you.* I could read and understand the words in Spanish, but that was it. I couldn't say them back.

I'd been to Sadie's house many times before, but I'd never stayed overnight. My mom had an aversion to sleepovers, but this time my dad had intervened and let me come.

The gleaming surfaces of the Merrill residence took my breath away. Everything was minimalistic and clean. Even the mudroom, which connected the garage to the main house, was all straight lines and white surfaces.

Clara headed straight to Sadie's suite, and Sadie followed her mom to the kitchen. Not knowing where to go, I followed the flow of the house until I stopped at the only cluttered area, the main entrance, which was being remodeled.

The addition of a mural of a tree superimposed on a world map took up the whole wall. I'd seen sketches of it but not the whole thing. I tried to make sense of myriad small pictures and names that dotted the area of Western Europe and Scandinavia, and a single pictureless name that appeared in the southern US and one in northern Africa. Colorful pins covered the world map.

Seeing the old-fashioned pictures, I got the gist of it: the pictures over Europe were Sadie's ancestors. This was the Merrill family tree. A lot of families in our area were into genealogy, but the Merrills had taken their game to the next level. They were obsessed. I never envied Sadie because her family was rich, but now I felt a twinge inside me. I too would've loved to have generations of family history. Unfortunately, when my mom's family had moved from Argentina, a lot stayed behind, including nonessentials—old pictures and the things that couldn't be packed, like history and memories. I'd never have a family tree like this.

I looked at the names underneath the pictures and found Sadie's. Sadie Lynn Merrill, the youngest of eight kids.

But if this was a family tree, what about the spots in America and Africa? And what about the pins?

Tasha walked into the entrance, and yelped.

"Sorry!" I exclaimed, my face flaming. Maybe I wasn't supposed to be here.

Tasha's eyes softened, and before I knew it, she was hugging me. "My sweetheart! You just scared me! I thought everyone had gone upstairs to Sadie's suite!" Her huge breasts, unnaturally hard, pressed against my shoulder, but I didn't know how to wiggle out of her embrace without offending her.

Finally she let go, and with a bright expression said, "Our brand-new family tree. We just finished it. What do you think?"

"It's cool."

Unfazed by my lack of enthusiasm, she added, "These are all our ancestors. From the British Isles but also from Sweden and Denmark." She pointed at a name and the picture of a young man of dark hair and eyes and said, "And probably the reason for our dark hair, my Italian great-great-grandfather."

At least something I had in common with them. "Oh, my great-grandparents were from Italy too."

Tasha's eyes widened, and she pursed her lips. "Really? I wouldn't have guessed!"

I waved a hand in front of my face. "Well, there's a big Italian influence in Argentina."

That's what my parents said all the time. My mom's maiden name was Rossi.

But Tasha seemed genuinely surprised. "Really? But you have a lot of native . . . roots too, right?"

So, in my family we always talked about the cool European ancestors, but never about our Native Argentine ones. Why didn't we, though? My sister, with her dark skin and hair, was definitely South American–looking. She'd even been invited to participate in a movie about the first inhabitants of the Americas. She'd said no.

"I guess," I said, and Tasha smiled, as if she were relieved for some reason.

After a couple of seconds of silence, I asked, "What about the names in America and in Africa?"

Tasha beamed at me. Apparently, I'd asked the perfect question, the one she was bursting to answer. "See? We did — I mean, *I* did the DNA test, the kind where you send your saliva to be analyzed, and it turns out I have a full four percent of Native blood, Cherokee, and guess what? Two percent North African! I was so touched that I have some diversity in me! *Our* family is diverse, though. A lot of my nieces and nephews are adopted. Such a labor of love to bring these less fortunate kids into our blessed family, you know?"

She sounded so excited, I resisted the urge to explain the fallacy of those percentages or comment anything on the kids. I'd never met Sadie's cousins and she never talked about them.

Tasha continued explaining, "The pins are the missionaries from our family who've gone to serve all over the world. Sadie's dad served in Mexico. We love our little brothers and sisters in Mexico. They're so innocent and giving! They're poor but happy, you know?"

I didn't know how to respond to that. Thankfully, Sadie came to the rescue. "There you are!" She hugged me just like Tasha had hugged me before, and then she looked at Tasha and said, "Mom, Rory —"

A crash drowned the rest of her words.

Tasha ran toward the sound, and Sadie and I followed her to the garage.

At the mudroom entrance, Sadie's dad stood holding two plastic bags that had given way. A smattering of glass covered the floor, and my and Clara's bags. He was a large, red-faced man with sparse blond hair. I'd met him before, but briefly.

Now he shook his head like a small child, and said, "I wanted to bring the drinks in for burgers tonight. The bags tore before I could catch the bottles."

Tasha slapped her hand against her thigh, just like my mom did when she was frustrated. "Didn't Manuela bring those in earlier today? What do I pay her for if she's not going to do her job right?" Her voice was so shrill I had to resist the urge to cover my ears.

Sadie didn't hesitate, though. "Well, Mom, by the looks of it, no, she didn't, but that's not the point now, is it?"

She took the plastic bags from her dad's hands and said, "Careful. Don't cut yourself."

Her dad muttered something under his breath, and seeing a broom by the door, I grabbed it and started sweeping the glass, gathering it in a tiny mountain.

"Thank you, sweetheart!" Tasha said. "I'm glad you know how to do this. Manuela isn't coming until Monday! It'll all be sticky until then! The ants . . ."

Sadie helped her dad out and he walked inside. When I finished sweeping, I looked for a cleaning closet. Given how organized this house was, it was intuitive that there would be one near the mudroom. At the third door I tried, I found a closet with cleaning supplies lined up like in a store. I ignored the stash of *Clean Up America* signs in a corner, but still, I wondered why they'd put them in the cleaning closet. I grabbed all-purpose cleaner and a couple of rags, and cleaned the floor. In no time, it looked like no soda had spilled.

"It's like magic," Sadie's dad said, standing next to me, holding a bunch of paper towels. "Sadie wouldn't know what to do. I guess it's in the blood, right?"

Sadie looked at me in a time-stopping way, and she seemed to beg me to just ignore him. I smiled, and said, "Thank you," choosing kindness, like the slogans said at school. It had been a compliment of sorts. Kind of.

Tasha came with a spray bottle that looked like it contained glass cleaner, judging by the blue product, and seeing the clean floor, she said, "Wow! This is impressive. Thanks, Rory. Linden, remember Rory, Sadie's Spanish friend? What a sweetheart, right?"

"Spanish?" he asked, a look of surprise overtaking his face. "But your English's perfect!"

This wasn't the first time I'd met him or that he'd told me this either, so I knew what to say. "I was born in Salt Lake City. I've lived in Utah all my life. My mom's from Argentina."

"Right!" he said. "Of course, I remember you! I went to Buenos Aires last month. Beautiful place to do business." Sadie's dad smiled at me, but I didn't know what to say to that. I'd never been to Buenos Aires. He pointed at the bags, soaking with red sticky soda, and said, "Thanks for cleaning, but too bad whatever was in that bag is dirty."

"Oh, I'm sure it's okay," I said, but when I checked the contents, glad to change the subject, I saw that indeed, my sleeping T-shirt and other stuff were sticky with soda. At least my phone was in my shorts' back pocket.

"Let me take care of that," said Tasha, grabbing my stuff. "Go shower. You must be all scratchy after getting out of that disgusting chlorinated water. I'll bring you and Clara something to wear."

"Follow me," Sadie said, and led me to her room, which was, like her mother had called it earlier, a whole suite. My house wasn't humble in the least, but Sadie's room was bigger than my whole first floor.

Clara was watching videos on Sadie's computer, as comfortable as if she were at home. Sadie explained what had happened to our stuff, and said Clara could shower in the guest room. "You can go in my bathroom, Rory."

Clara looked crestfallen, like I'd scored against her, but when Sadie explained I'd helped clean up the mess with the soda, she didn't complain.

"Sadie! Come down for a second," Tasha called from the intercom.

"I'll be right back," Sadie said. "My bathroom is through that door."

"Okay," I said, and once she ran downstairs, I headed to the bathroom.

My body shivered with pleasure at the most luxurious shower of my life. I tried a couple of sugar scrubs and body washes from the shelf in the enormous shower. I hoped Sadie wouldn't mind. The glass of the windows and walls fogged up with the steam, and when someone cracked the door open, a tendril of cold air tickled my feet.

"I'm leaving underwear and a T-shirt here!" Sadie called.

I was moved that she cared so much. I hadn't had a friend like her since ... Nano. The feeling of loss enveloped me again, but I threw it down the drain along with the most prickling comments by Sadie's parents. They seemed like such nice people. They didn't mean to sound so . . .

Racist, the word came to my mind, and embarrassed, I spoke aloud. "Stop it, Aurora!"

If Sadie heard my thoughts, she'd be so hurt. She didn't deserve it.

When I turned off the water, I wrapped myself in one of the fluffiest towels I'd ever touched. It was warm and I realized the towel rack was heated. I wrapped my hair with a smaller towel. I'd have to braid my hair so it wouldn't frizz up worse than dandelion fluff. Tomorrow, I'd have to flat-iron it before heading down to see the family again. Sadie hadn't seen me with curly hair in years.

I picked up the red T-shirt from the floor, and when I opened it up to put it on, the shock of seeing the words printed across the front froze my hands.

I dropped it. The shirt landed on a small puddle of water at my feet.

Clean Up America.

The words were imprinted on my eyes.

I blinked a few times to erase them, but when I picked up the T-shirt again, the words were still there.

Clean Up America was the winning slogan of the

current president of the country. During the national elections, the country was torn apart as one candidate urged his followers to clean up America, to get rid of the garbage, the gays, the Asians, but especially the Hispanics and the Blacks. My mom said the slogan was just as evil as the Nazi swastika.

Although I never got involved in politics, my mom was an engaged activist and attended marches and rallies to protest against racism and oppression. My dad didn't attend the marches, but he was vocally opposed to the regime, as he called it.

My mom and my sister would be getting posters ready for the pro-immigrant march tomorrow at the Salt Lake City capitol. My mom always said that although we weren't in danger of deportation, we were still affected by the anti-immigrant sentiment. She raged against the people in our church who wouldn't get involved, claiming they weren't immigrants, or that they didn't want to offend anyone. Kids in cages, crying for their parents, was a human rights issue, she said, and until the injustices against them stopped, then no one would be free of blame.

I couldn't wear this shirt.

Wearing it would be going against my family values, against everything I'd been taught to cherish.

Wearing it would be sending a big F-You to my parents' sacrifices as immigrants in America. To my ancestors running from war, hunger, and strife. The only difference between some of my ancestors and Sadie's was that mine landed south of the equator.

But if I didn't wear the T-shirt, then Sadie would be offended.

She had to have other shirts for me to wear. Did she pick this one by accident? Didn't she realize what a position she'd put me in?

"Are you okay?" Sadie's soft voice asked from behind the door. "I've been knocking and I'm wondering . . ."

Sweat beads covered my upper lip and I wiped them off with the fluffy towel. The smell of chlorine leftover on my skin made me sneeze.

"Yes," I said, wrapping the towel around my body. "Sadie . . . there's a problem."

It was now or never. I pushed down on the long door handle and peeked my head out of the door. In a corner of the room, Clara sat eating a burger. She wore the same red *Clean Up America* T-shirt I was supposed to wear.

"What's wrong?" Sadie asked, still in her soft voice.

My gaze flitted to her. Her wet brown hair fell on her shoulders, and there was a curl I had never noticed before. Sadie too wore the red shirt.

I gathered strength, and said, "Sadie, I mean . . . don't be mad at me, but I can't wear this."

Confusion flashed in her eyes. "Is it too small? They're all large, my mom said. They're comfy."

So her mom had given her the T-shirts. Sadie wasn't

trying to play me. But now, how could I explain so she'd understand?

"See? I can't wear a shirt with this slogan." I bit my lip and laughed nervously. "My mom will literally disown me."

"For a T-shirt?" Sadie asked.

There was a long, heavy silence I wished I didn't have to fill.

Finally, I said, "If I were Jewish, would you ask me to wear a Hitler T-shirt? One with the swastika?"

By now, Clara had paused the video she'd been watching. An argument between Sadie and me was the best entertainment she could've hoped for. To make matters worse, Tasha stepped into the room.

She scanned the situation, as if sensing trouble. She looked ready to pounce to stop whatever it was that was making Sadie unhappy.

"Are you really comparing our president to Hitler?" Sadie asked.

She'd never talked about the president. I'd been under the impression that since the president's policies didn't affect her negatively, that she had no idea who the president was. Or that at least she shared my dislike of him. Now, I wasn't a militant against him like my mom was, but I didn't like the guy. I hadn't liked him even when he was just the host of bad reality TV.

Judging by Sadie's reaction, she knew who he was and she was ready to defend him because I'd compared him to Hitler.

My ears started ringing. Even my lips tingled. I wasn't used to speaking up.

"Well . . . He's not that popular, right?" I said, my voice shaky.

"For *your people* I guess not," Tasha said, cutting into the conversation.

What did she mean by *your people*? Immigrants in general? Undocumented immigrants? Latinos? Hispanics like Tasha kept calling anyone who spoke Spanish or had roots south of the Rio Grande?

I didn't want a fight. I just didn't want to wear the shirt.

Sadie turned around to face her mom and said, "Rory says her mom will kill her if she wears this T-shirt." I couldn't see her face, but I heard the eye rolling in her voice.

Clara looked like one of the hyenas from *The Lion King*, licking their lips at the carnage in front of them.

"Well then, you don't have to tell her," Tasha said, without a hint of sympathy in her face or voice. "How will she know you're wearing it?"

My ears kept ringing and my breath hitched in my throat.

"Keep it between us. She'll never know," Tasha added, and then she turned around to look at Clara and said, "Don't post anything in your Snapchats or Instagrams or whatever, and that's it."

The three of them looked at me as if the issue had been settled.

"I . . . I can't," I said.

Tasha sighed, snatched the T-shirt from my hand, and turned it over inside out. She gave it back to me and said, "Geez, Rory. I never intended . . ." Her voice shook, and her eyes filled with tears. "I thought the cotton was comfy for a sleep shirt."

I clutched the shirt against my chest, feeling guilty that she was on the verge of tears.

"I'm sorry," I said. Wearing the T-shirt inside out was a perfectly logical situation, right? My mom didn't have to know.

Sadie walked up to her mom and hugged her. Tasha kissed the top of Sadie's head, and looking at me with sad eyes said, "You know, I never see color when I see you. You're a good friend to Sadie, and I like you. I never considered your parents' ideologies. I am of the belief that when adults' problems get involved in kids' relationships, then things go wrong. Sorry." She stretched out her hand to take the shirt again. "You know what? If it makes you so uncomfortable, don't wear it. I'm sorry for thinking this wasn't an issue at all."

"The thing is," I said, surprising even myself, "the president's views against immigrants are offensive—"

"But you're not an immigrant," Sadie exclaimed.

"My mom is," I said.

Tasha shook her head and said, "No, you're misinterpreting his words. They're taken out of context by the fake media. He doesn't mean immigrants like your mother!" She laughed but the sound chilled me. "He means the illegals. They come to our country and steal our jobs and live off the government. I mean, we need rules, right?"

I hated confrontations. I hated having to defend my ideas.

"I'm sorry," I said again. Something in my voice must have told her she'd won. They'd won.

"Don't make a big deal out of this, Rory," Tasha said in a honeyed voice. "Your clothes will be dry in a few minutes, and if you're uncomfortable, you can change back into them."

Clara ran to Tasha's side, and Tasha said in a loud whisper that carried to me, "I never meant to offend her. I'm sorry. I'm not a monster." She cried, and Sadie went to her mom too.

In the bathroom, I put on the shirt, inside out. The letters didn't burn my skin. There was no magical property to them, but they still had power.

Clean Up America meant that the country, with all

the undesirable people, was dirty. That even though I passed as white, I too was part of the problem.

I stared at myself in the mirror. Why was I wearing this shirt? My silence made *me* the problem.

Why had I said I was sorry? Why was Tasha the victim now?

But then, why hadn't I just put the shirt on to start with and avoided this issue? If my mom saw a picture, I could explain. She would be furious, but she was my mom. She'd understand when I explained that I was practically in a no-win situation.

I walked back into the room, and the atmosphere was still chilly and weird, even though I ate the burgers Sadie's dad had cooked, and I watched *La La Land* like Sadie wanted. When Clara brought up the topic that people on Twitter complained about the movie, Sadie made a face of disgust and said, "People complain about everything. Everything is about race. *They* create the problems, right?" She looked at me, and I nodded.

Silent.

Every cell in me screamed that they were wrong, but I didn't speak up.

A couple of times, Sadie tried to start a conversation with me, pretending nothing had happened. It always ended up on Nano, and I wondered, had she only invited me to learn more about him?

When I went to check if my clothes were dry — they weren't — and came back to the room, I caught the tail end of a conversation. I stood outside of the door to overhear.

"Maybe she wants to keep him for herself," Clara said.

"Why would she do that?" Sadie asked.

Clara laughed and whispered loudly enough for me to hear from outside of the room, "They're both Mexicans, you know? Their people are attracted to their same kind. I can't understand how you can have a crush on him, Sadie. I would never . . . Besides, he had a rainbow bracelet. I bet he's gay."

I walked into the room and they continued playing Uno and laughing like they hadn't been gossiping about me and Nano. I didn't even know how to start telling them all that was wrong in their conversation, and I ached for a friend who'd understand what I was feeling even when I didn't understand myself.

At night, in the top bunk in Sadie's guest quarters, I couldn't sleep. I still wanted to take off the shirt and burn it. I wanted to run home. And once the thought took root in my mind, it didn't let go.

Go home. Go home, my heart chanted.

Clara and Sadie slept soundly, while in my mind, I went over the incident at the pool, then cleaning up the soda, the T-shirt, the overheard conversation. All the words that had vanished from my tongue came back to me in a rush. They circled in my head like fish in a too-small tank.

Go home. Go home, my heart said again.

How many times had random people in the streets told my mom to go home when she marched for freedom and equality? Once I'd asked her why she kept marching if there was no positive consequence that I could see. She'd told me that when one group was oppressed and persecuted, no one was really free, that she hadn't understood that when she was younger. Now she knew better. There was no room for silence.

Tonight, I'd been silent.

Now I wanted to go home.

But if I did just what the *Clean Up America* crowd demanded, if I went home, I'd lose Sadie's friendship forever. And if I walked out on her right now, I'd have to walk out on so many people, and the mere thought of it was already exhausting.

When I was eight years old, Nano's mom and my mom had a small argument. A disagreement, I should say. I didn't know what it was about back in those days, but I remember the scary feeling that settled on Nano and me as we played Mario Kart, hearing our moms arguing in loud voices. Ale, Nano's brother, had been in his room all day. He was thirteen at the time.

That's the last time I went to their house. At first, I'd asked why I couldn't see Nano, and my mom avoided answering. Until Marina broke it down for me. Nano's mom had told our mom that Alejandro was gay and invited our mom to a march. My mom had said no, that she wasn't comfortable with the idea. That she loved Ale, but there were things with *that lifestyle* that she didn't agree with.

Nano's mom erased my mom and our family from their lives. My mom had been devastated, but she'd never tried to explain face-to-face. She'd never spoken up to admit she'd been wrong.

The friendship died.

And now in bed, wearing this hated T-shirt, I realized any crumb of friendship I'd had with Sadie had died too. When Tasha and Sadie claimed they didn't see color, they acted as if my family and culture were just skin-deep, that because I passed for what they called *white*, I could shed the parts of me that couldn't be assimilated. But maybe I had contributed to this too, believing that if I ignored the parts of me they didn't like, I could pretend their words and actions to *my people* didn't hurt. I contained multitudes, and wearing the T-shirt, I betrayed the parts of me no eye could see, the ones that in the end mattered the most.

I sat up in bed, the words too powerful to drown in sleep.

In silence, I texted my truest friend for a ride and gathered my clothes from the dryer. I took off the horrible

T-shirt, folded it, and placed it on the bed. Without a backward glance, I walked out of Sadie's suite, downstairs, to the front door, relieved that I wasn't killing my soul just to belong. The price for playing the game was just too much.

Just before I opened the door, Sadie called out, "Rory, where are you going?"

With my heart in my mouth, I turned around to face her. She walked downstairs and looked at me like I was the one who had betrayed our friendship. "Why are you leaving?"

Did she really want to know?

"Sadie," I said, and this time, the words didn't stick to the roof of my mouth. "Why am I your friend? How are you my friend?"

She stared at me. "Is this still about the shirt?"

My silence was loud between us.

"Clara was right — you're so extra." Her arms crossed on her chest like a shield showed me that words could never reach her.

Maybe with time. Maybe one day she would understand what I meant. But not now. Now she wouldn't understand. We had no common ground.

"I lied before," I said. "I'm not sorry for speaking up. In fact, I'm tired of not saying more. Enough, Sadie. No more. You hurt me today, and I'm not being extra, and if you can't see that, if you don't understand how you've hurt me, then how can you be my friend?"

She didn't say anything, but at least she didn't cry.

I walked out of her house, and I waited on the dark sidewalk, Sadie's mansion looming behind me. The sprinklers awakened the green and luscious smell of the night.

Nano's car arrived a few seconds later, and I got in, and the car smelled of safety, of my childhood.

"Are you okay?" he asked, and in his eyes, there was so much understanding.

I told him everything. Everything that had happened tonight, and everything that had happened before, with my mom. Of how she missed Nano's mom. How she'd changed and now attended marches for rights for all.

The sun peeked out from behind Mount Timpanogos. The dawn was always my favorite part of the day. Aurora in Spanish means dawn. After a night of agony, I wanted to be rising too, but I didn't know how.

Nano listened to my words in silence, but the companionable, understandable kind, and when we parked at my house, he smiled and said, "Nice!"

"You should come over. My mom would love to see you," I said.

He smiled again, and I pressed his hand.

"I'll tell my mom she should call your mom. Time doesn't really heal if there's silence, you know?" I said.

I kissed his cheek and got out of the car. He waited for me until I opened the door of my house and walked in. There was no giant family tree, or missionary pins on the wall, but here, I didn't have to pretend my history didn't matter.

I sat on my bed watching the newborn sun. Sadie might not have completely understood my words. Tasha and Clara might add their interpretation once Sadie told them what I'd said. But I'd spoken up for myself. They were not holding my head down underwater anymore. I wasn't going to drown.

A balloon of light swelled inside me, and I savored the feeling. I had thought I didn't know how to rise, but when I stood in front of Sadie and told her how I felt? That was me, rising to the world.

RUTH

BY LAURA SILVERMAN

MY PHONE PINGS SIX TIMES in a row, then seven, then eight. Excited, I quickly close out of the page on the computer screen, where my latest blog post, "Fifteen Feminist as Heck YA Books," just went live. Then I pick up my phone. The screen lights up with a flood of notifications from Twitter, where all of my blog content auto-posts. I spin around in Mom's office chair and kick my feet up on the computer desk while reading the comments, barely finishing one before another arrives.

Bookish-Boy12: Omg these recs are perfect *TBR explodes*

Rosa-Diaz-Forever: Why do you keep doing this to my wallet?

Authoring-Always: Thanks for including me, Ruth!

I glow with pride as all the comments pour in. I spend a lot of time on my blog posts (too much time, according to my dad, even though he's the one who drives me to the bookstore and library whenever I want), so it's always heartening to know people appreciate the work.

As I'm about to start replying to the comments, my phone buzzes with a text from Daniel. We met online in the blogging community last year and immediately bonded over our love for YA books with Jewish characters, a subgenre that can be frustratingly scant.

Have you seen this? Daniel asks.

He attaches an article link. Something about an adoption agency in Georgia refusing to let Jewish and Muslim couples adopt children and Congress allowing it. My skin crawls just reading it. What's wrong with people?

That's bullshit! I text back.

I read the article, all my book-blogging joy evaporating and quickly being replaced with anger. My parents always talk about politics. I used to zone them out, but now there's an election in one month and with my eighteenth birthday two weeks before that, I'll be able to vote for the first time. I should probably start paying more attention.

I tweet the article link and caption it: "Congress is trying to ban Jewish and Muslim couples from adopting babies!! #VoteThemOut."

I sigh and run a hand through my hair. Blech. My curls are tangled and matted after a particularly sweaty tennis practice. It's late. I need to jump in the shower and go to sleep before my parents tell me to jump in the shower and go to sleep.

Twenty minutes later, I'm in my own room, in bed with the latest book from my TBR pile and brushing my wet hair with one hand so I can read at the same time. Just as I'm turning a page, my phone pings. Then pings again and again and again. Probably more likes on my blog post!

I scan the notifications, brow furrowing. The messages are from unfamiliar users and all replying to my adoption tweet. I lean forward and read a couple tweets.

BlueWave-2020: #VoteThemOut

Dems-4-Life: Shame on them!

I smile, glad to see I spread the word. I'm about to put my phone down and go back to reading when one more message pings in.

Pepe-Lover: Shut up Jew.

My stomach drops, throat tightens. The words stare me down.

Shut up Jew, Shut up Jew, Shut up Jew.

It's a troll. Just a stupid troll. I've had them before on my blog posts, particularly the feminist ones like the one tonight. They call me silly or ridiculous, or, most ironically, *sexist*. But never this — no one has ever mentioned my religion — not on my roundup of books with the best Shabbat dinner scenes and not in my post comparing YA characters to the characters in *Fiddler on the Roof.*

My fingers hesitate. Do I respond? Quote-tweet with something strong and pithy like I do with the feminist trolls? Make sure my followers see the comment so they can rally behind me?

Shut up Jew, Shut up Jew, Shut up Jew.

I live near Atlanta. There are a lot of Jewish people in my community, even at my public school. We don't deal with anti-Semitism. I've never dealt with anti-Semitism.

Jew.

Suddenly the word I've identified with my entire life feels dirty.

Another notification pings in. My heart skips a beat, and I swallow hard before reading it.

Endless-TBR: Definitely going to pick some of these books up! Thanks Ruth!

My body is tight, tense. *Jew.* I just want that word gone. Before I can overthink it, I block the troll, and then send out one more tweet before going to bed.

A few days later, I meet up with one of my real-life bookish friends at a little bookstore in Atlanta. There's a
reading and signing here today with one of our favorite
authors, but we're super early, so we decide to get coffee
down the block first. I still don't have my license because
Atlanta traffic is scary as heck, and okay, I'm maybe
more than a bit of a procrastinator, so my dad dropped
me off, and my friend is going to drive me home.

"Hmm, should I get caramel or double caramel?"
Kaitlyn asks me. She sweeps her blond hair over her
shoulder as she peruses the menu.

"Definitely double caramel," I respond, thinking I'll
have the same. We order and then step to the side to
wait for our drinks.

"Did you see the Twitter drama?" Kaitlyn asks.

Shut up Jew. For a moment, I think she's talking about
my Twitter drama, but there's no way anyone saw it that
quickly. Those three words still play over and over again
in my mind. Maybe I should have responded instead of
blocking him. Is that what he wanted? Or did he want to
scare me into silence? And do I care what he wanted? It
should be about what *I* wanted.

"Um, no," I say. "What's going on?"

"You haven't seen it? It's everywhere."

"I've been trying to stay off Twitter this week. . . ." I trail off, staring ahead.

"Ruth, you okay?"

Our drinks are ready, and Kaitlyn hands me mine. We walk over to the seating area and manage to grab two very cushy leather chairs. I curl up and take a sip of my drink, icy and sweet. Total perfection. Double caramel for the win.

"Um . . ." I play with the straw, bending it back and forth, before taking another sip. Should I tell Kaitlyn? She has a great Bookstagram, but she's quiet on Twitter and uses a cute little avatar as her profile picture. And, well, she isn't Jewish. I'm not sure if she'd understand, but still, it'd probably be smart to share what's going on with someone.

"Yeah, so," I say, fidgeting with my straw. "There was this troll on Twitter yesterday, and, um, he said shut up Jew?" I say it like a question, like I almost don't trust my own memory of what happened. Why didn't I take a screenshot? Will the message still be there if I unblock him? What if Kaitlyn doesn't believe me?

"What?" Kaitlyn exclaims. "Are you serious? That's disgusting, Ruth! We have to do something about it!"

"We do?" I ask.

"Of course! Can't let them get away with it. Let me see the tweet."

I wince. "I don't know if you can. I blocked him."

Kaitlyn gestures for my phone. I share the guy's username, and a second later, she has him unblocked, the tweet pulled up, and is ready to quote-tweet. "This is so gross," Kaitlyn says, shaking her head. "We'll tweet a great comeback and then have people report him for harassment, all right?"

I snort. "Yeah, because that always works so well. Twitter is terrible with harassment complaints."

"Yeah, but I bet if enough people do it, then it'll be more of a bother not to suspend the account. Okay, so . . ." Kaitlyn takes a minute to type out a response. She sips on her drink as she types, and sometimes the straw slips, making a loud slurping suctiony pop. "What about this?"

She passes me the phone, and I read the tweet. It's simple and clear. Still I'm unsure, but Kaitlyn's eyes are wide and excited. I nod and press post.

Bookish-Berkowitz: @Pepe-Lover Shut up Troll

"Pepe-Lover: Shut up Jew"

Raven-Puff-Girl: @Bookish-Berkowitz Omg!
Blocked and reported!

Unrequited-For-Molly: @Bookish-Berkowitz
@Pepe-Lover Go back to your cave of
deplorables, pepe!

"Wow, that's a lot of responses," Kaitlyn says as we leave the bookstore. The event was really awesome and got my mind off things for a bit. The author ran late, but she was the sweetest and apologized a million times and stayed to sign everyone's books even though the line was like two hours long.

I clutch my precious signed copy to my chest, excited to Instagram it and the stack of three other books I couldn't resist picking up while at the store. I open my tote bag and sniff the rest of my stash. Mmm. There is nothing better than the smell of brand-new books. Except perhaps the delicious scent of used books. Basically, all book smells are great, and I finally need to give in and buy a book-scented candle.

"You've got to look at this," Kaitlyn continues, passing me her phone. I sigh. Can't I keep this book high a little bit longer?

But I glance at the screen, and my mouth drops open. Forty-three retweets and over a hundred responses? I never get this kind of traction. Quickly, I check my own account and find that two big authors and an editor I adore retweeted the post. And also —

"Omg!" I squeal. "Read The Force followed me!"

@Read-The-Force is a huge book blogger. I've been watching their YouTube videos for years. My fingers hover over the DM button, but I resist. If I fangirl all up in their face, I might scare them off.

"Ahh! And look," Kaitlyn says, leaning into me and sharing her own screen again. "The troll's account has been suspended. Awesome new followers and suspended account. Not bad for a day's work, huh?"

"Not bad," I reply.

Kaitlyn knocks shoulders with me. "C'mon, you can keep scrolling while I drive. Gotta get home for dinner, or I'll never hear the end of it from Dad, who thinks he's God's gift for cooking once a week. Read comments to me while I drive?"

"Sure thing!"

Later that night, after I've finished my pile of homework for school tomorrow, I'm in bed and texting with Daniel. We're reading the same book right now, which means reading is going slowly because we stop at the end of each chapter and text each other all of our feels.

Okay, okay, back to reading. Btw, that's awesome about the total troll domination. Sorry that happened to you!

Thanks! Just some weird freak thing I guess. Okay, back to reading!

I'm only a page into the next chapter when my phone buzzes again. I roll my eyes, grinning, because Daniel always has a final thing to say. I swear the sequel is going to be out by the time we finish this book. But it's not Daniel. It's a Twitter notification.

Pepe-Reborn: Can't get rid of me that easily, K*ke

My heart races as I stare at the word, a slur I've only heard about in Hebrew School classes. And who are all of those people he's tagging? I go to text Kaitlyn for advice, but suddenly my phone buzzes again and again and again. My eyes widen as notifications flood in. Five retweets of the troll's tweet, then twelve, then seventeen, then twenty-six. How is it multiplying so fast? Who retweeted him?

I check one of the tagged accounts and see they retweeted the post to 430,000 followers. Panic courses through me as responses flood in. More slurs and hateful comments and pictures also. A cartoon illustration of that Pepe frog standing outside of a concentration camp. And then . . . and then real photos of concentration camps. Starved bodies and sunken eyes.

Bile rises in the back of my throat, and I swallow hard. I don't want to look at this. I can't look at this. Hands shaking, I put my account on lock, but some of the trolls have already followed me. Not knowing what else to do, I disable my account.

Silence.

Then my phone buzzes again.

I jump. How are they still getting to me? Heart in my throat, I turn my phone over and glance at the screen with one eye.

Daniel

DID YOU FINISH THE CHAPTER? Omg THAT KISS.

I hesitate, unsure whether or not to tell him about what just happened. He's Jewish. He would probably understand more than anyone else in the community. And he'll notice my account is disabled eventually. But those pictures flash before my eyes — gaunt, tortured people. Not just people but relatives of mine. All of my family was from Europe at one point or another. Cousins of cousins of cousins. They were from Europe, and now they're not anywhere.

I push the thought away and text back:

> Haha yeah great kiss

Great? Omg I thought it was so awk!

> Uh I meant great in its awkwardness.
> I'm gonna go to bed. Read more tomorrow!

I put my phone down, hoping disabling my account was the right call. They're just bored internet people trying to bait me. They can't win if I'm not online. I distract myself with my bedtime routine. I have a test at school tomorrow and a tennis match later in the day. I need to concentrate, focus. Shower, stretch, brush my hair. When I get back into bed, I automatically go to open Twitter. Right, can't do that. Instead, I go to my blog and read all the comments on my latest post. Maybe being off Twitter for a bit will be good. I'll have more time to attack my TBR. I can get another post up sooner. I click off my screen and go to sleep.

My dreams are scattered that night. There's darkness and shouting and running and hiding. I wake up before dawn, sweating and with all of my sheets kicked off. I try to shake off the feeling as I get ready, showering again to get off the dried sweat and making a treat-yourself breakfast of peanut butter–banana toast drizzled with honey. By the time I'm at school, my thoughts are focused back on class, with only the remnants of the dream still clinging to them.

At lunch that afternoon, I'm sitting next to Kaitlyn and a bunch of other friends. The cafeteria is packed and as loud as ever, people shouting across the table to get each other's attention.

"Isn't this adorable?" Kaitlyn asks, showing me her screen. "I'm so good at Bookstagram, it's honestly unbelievable."

I snort. "Low self-confidence much?"

But I oblige and glance at the screen as Kaitlyn scrolls through a dozen photos, pointing out her favorite. "I think the orange cover really pops in this one," she says. "But the FunkoPop is out of frame." She twists her lips. "Hmm, what do you think?"

"This one for sure," I say, pointing to another photo where the crispness and saturation is so perfect Apple could probably use it for an advertisement.

"Perfect!" Kaitlyn grins and starts tapping away.

I take a bite of my congealed mashed potatoes. Mmm. I will never admit to anyone how much I love cold, clumped, congealed cafeteria mashed potatoes. I'm a freak, and I know it.

". . . yeah, but Jewish people are rich."

My shoulders tense. I keep looking down at my mashed

potatoes, listening in on the conversation happening farther down the table. A quick glance to the left tells me it's two guys from my biology class. I haven't had much overlap with them and can't recall their names.

"That's because they make all that money in Hollywood and keep it for themselves."

"Must be nice. Maybe I should marry a Jewish girl one day."

In this moment, I'm overtly aware of my thick, curly brown hair, of the small Star of David pendant I've worn around my neck since my bat mitzvah, of my absences from school this past month for Rosh Hashanah and Yom Kippur. I stare down at my congealed mashed potatoes, my stomach in knots.

Shut up Jew.

Can't get rid of me that easily, K*ke.

Those are threats. Those are slurs.

They make all that money in Hollywood and keep it for themselves.

What is that? An assumption? A bias? Prejudice?

It definitely isn't true. My parents don't work in Hollywood, and they donate more to charity than anyone else I know. It's called tzedakah. It's our responsibility to give back.

"Ruth, why haven't you liked my post yet?" Kaitlyn asks.

I turn to her and keep my voice low. "Did you hear them say that?"

"Huh? Who? Say what?"

Kaitlyn, opposite of covertly, whips her head back and forth, looking at everyone at our long table. I shove her gently in the side with my elbow. "Stop looking around," I say. "Look at me, and *quiet*. Those two guys at the left end of the table. They were talking about . . . they were . . ." I pause. "They said like all Jews work in Hollywood."

Kaitlyn pauses, blinks, then shrugs. "Yeah, I mean a lot of them do, don't they?"

My throat tightens. Suddenly, I feel hot and itchy and like I want to cry right here in the cafeteria in front of everyone and my congealed mashed potatoes. This is Kaitlyn. My friend who told me to go after the anti-Semitic troll. But now something is happening in real life, and she doesn't think anything of it? Does she . . . does she think it's true?

"My parents don't work in Hollywood. . . ." I say quietly.

The bell rings, and everyone gets up, grabbing their trays and backpacks. Kaitlyn glances back and smiles brightly to me as we exit the cafeteria. "Be sure to like my Instagram!"

And then she turns, and we walk down opposite hallways.

I flip through the pages until I find the quote I want. Last year I read this memoir by a Holocaust survivor,

Elie Wiesel's *Night*, to write my "5 Jewish Nonfiction Must-Reads" list, and there was this quote that's always stuck with me. . . .

There it is, the quote I circled, then highlighted, then starred. "Neutrality helps the oppressor, never the victim. Silence encourages the tormentor, never the tormented."

The thing is, I thought those internet trolls were just that, internet trolls. Ignore them, and they'll go away. But it's like all of their vitriol is bleeding into real life or something. Because maybe if something is repeated enough times, even from an unreliable source like a troll online, it sinks in, and a lie slowly becomes the truth. And maybe if teenage boys scrolling on Twitter or Reddit hear it enough times, they'll begin to believe it, and they won't even think twice when they mention it at a cafeteria table. And maybe if no one speaks up to those guys at a cafeteria table, they'll grow up and become politicians, and they won't see anything wrong about voting for laws not allowing us to adopt from certain places because to be honest they've always heard bad things about those Jews.

I should have responded to Kaitlyn in the cafeteria today. I should have made her listen when I said my parents don't work in Hollywood, and I should have explained why the idea we all do feels insidious. And I should have asked her to stand up for and with me and confront those guys.

Because when I read a book with horrible representation, whether it's ableist or racist or fatphobic, I tweet and blog about it, making sure everyone I can reach hears me. I stand up for what's right. So why have I not been doing that for myself?

I snap a photo of the quote.

Then I text Daniel:

> Hey, can you help me with something?

Six hours later, my eyes are burning from staring at a computer screen for so long, and my hands are shaking from weariness, nerves, and excitement. The post is beautiful. My very best yet. I told Daniel everything that happened, and he helped me comb the shelves to put this together. This could go badly. The trolls could take things even further, leave comments on my actual blog or even hack my email.

But I can't let them stay out there alone, saying these hateful and false things, without someone countering them. Because if they're the only voice out there, then they are right by default.

Daniel texts me:

> Post it already!

My finger wavers above the key for just a moment.
Shut up Jew. Shut up Jew. Shut up Jew.
I hit post.

Not Your Jewish Stereotype: 15 Books Featuring Glorious Jewish Heroes and Heroines

Dear Readers —

As some of you might have noticed, I disabled my Twitter account for a short time. That is because after tweeting about a potential law impacting Jewish people's ability to adopt children (linked here), I was targeted by an anti-Semitic troll. When I fought back, the troll brought in the cavalry and flooded my account with hateful threats and photos. I thought it was best to delete my account, to not give them the satisfaction of response.

But I was wrong. Because as Elie Wiesel, renowned Holocaust survivor, said, "Neutrality helps the oppressor, never the victim. Silence encourages the tormentor, never the tormented."

If I let the trolls be the only voices out there, then they will win. So I will not encourage their hatefulness with my silence. Instead, I will fight back by promoting the heck out of some incredible Jewish books. Buy these books, read these books, and follow the Jewish tradition of tzedakah and donate these books so others can enjoy and learn from them.

Jewish people are not evil. Or less than. And we are not one thing. We are not all lawyers or bankers — or all working in Hollywood. As you read this selection of books, you will learn, however, that many of us are kind, and passionate, and giving.

Thank you for reading this post. I would be so grateful if you shared it.

Yours,

Ruth Berkowitz

Kaitlyn finds me in the hall the next day at school. "I'm the worst, aren't I?" she asks as she grabs my arm and leans into me.

I pause before responding. "You are definitely not *the* worst."

Last night and this morning there was a lot of *the* worst. That's because I reactivated my Twitter and not only posted my latest blog post but also tagged all of the trolls in it. There was a war in my mentions. Terrible comments and threats from the trolls but then also what felt like the whole bookish community fighting back at them. @Read-The-Force even quote-tweeted it with a whole beautiful thread of anger and love. I had no idea they were Jewish also. The post was every-where, and all of these people messaged with screen-shots of their book orders.

So Kaitlyn definitely isn't the worst, but what she said did hurt.

"I'm sorry," Kaitlyn says. "Really and truly. I wasn't thinking yesterday."

"Thank you for apologizing." I hesitate. "I guess that's part of it — you weren't thinking. It's kind of upsetting those subconscious thoughts are already in your head."

Kaitlyn blinks hard. "I know. It's weird and bad, and I'm really sorry. I wanted to make it up to you, and you know, to just be better, so . . ." Kaitlyn pulls out her phone and shows me the screen. "I ran up to the bookstore last night after your post. They only had a few in stock, but . . ."

I look at the latest picture on Kaitlyn's Bookstagram. A stack of three glorious Jewish books from my list. The post already has hundreds of likes. "I have a couple more on order," she says. "And I'm going to totally read them! I promise these aren't just pretty shelf sitters."

I smile and say, "Thank you."

"Are we okay?" she asks.

"We're okay."

And we are okay. Because what she did hurt me, really hurt me, but she's here, and she's listening, and I know she'll work to do better. And that's what matters. Because yes, the trolls' voices are out there. But now those voices are being combated by @Read-The-Force's and Kaitlyn's and those of fifteen incredible Jewish writers — and also, my own voice.

I AM THE REVOLUTION

BY KEAH BROWN

I am alive
for now
I tried to kill me
before they ever could
so, now I write like
death is sitting on my porch swing
and he just invited himself in
but I'm not leaving this desk
until the story is done

I am alive
and screaming at the top of my lungs
Black Lives Matter
nothing about us without us
I am a feminist
I am whole

#DisabledAndCute
even like this
especially like this

I am alive
and proud
a little sensitive and angry
happy in my resistance
writing while death makes tea
we dance around each other
until he recedes

I am alive
I laugh and cry
sometimes the latter through the former
I dance around my living room
I sing in the car
I say my name like it's a love song
I smile at my reflection and tell her secrets

We are alive now
every single day of being
feels like a revolution

AS YOU WERE

BY BETHANY C. MORROW

I **LOVE BEING UNDER THE LIGHTS.** We all do. Being on the field, in a hyper-brightness that's sharp against the dark autumn night, we feel electrified. We even like that it's chilly, that there's a little bite to the air that keeps other people away.

Football practice has been over for hours before we arrive; the stadium is ours. The whole world is, and we're it.

A swath of hair is snatched from my lazy high knot by the same wind that immediately whips it around my face.

I don't react. I don't acknowledge that I was basically slapped in the face by hair so cold it feels like it's made of something sharper. I just mark time.

Jessie lifts her hands to amplify and I know the next round of commands is coming.

"To the right flank! To the left flank! To the right flank! To the right flank! Double to the rear!"

But she doesn't say the magic word, and the losers I hear take off behind me are met with shouts and jeers. They'll be the laughingstock for the next few seconds, just until they make it up to the stands and join the other disqualified band members. The chiding never lasts. Drill downs are how we unwind.

"As you were," Jessie bellows, and I wipe my brain clean, alternating from the ball of my right foot to the ball of my left as I mark time in wait.

The disqualified among the drumline are tapping out a metronome, but every so often a snare adds a ridiculous string of flourishes designed to energize everyone on the sidelines and maybe throw a few of us competitors off our game. We only compete against each other in this sacred space, alone beneath the lights, when we're pushing each other to be better. Because in the end, in the next field show competition or the next parade, it'll show. When it really counts, we'll win — or we won't — as one.

That's why I don't smile, even when Jessie accompanies the drumline by busting out pieces of her Mace Drum Major routine. Even when I wanna whoop and holler with the others because she placed first in our division last weekend, and she is a beast with that stick.

There's no inspection to pass during a drill down, but when I'm on, I'm on. My bandmates deserve that. So eyes forward, arms slightly bent, palms against my hips, middle fingers on the seam of my jeans. From the waist up, you can barely tell my feet are moving.

Jessie lifts her mace and the chatter dies down.

Here we go.

"To the rear, to the rear, to the right flank!" *Double to the rear, to the ri —* "To the left flank! High mark time!" She doesn't make us wait this time. "Hut!"

Step, pivot, step, pivot, step, turn, step, turn, and this is the part she'll drag out. Now we're marking time again, only instead of lifting our heels off the ground, we have to lift each foot knee-high. And keep time. Which, after three years of marching band, isn't a big deal. Unless for some reason I had to do it for two full minutes, *after* a longer-than-normal night of field show practice.

Jessie doesn't call out rest, so we keep going. A few people must be getting lazy because she stabs the air in their direction and they fall out.

I low-key hate high mark time. It's never a command given briefly. And it's really not hard, it just seems to double in intensity very quickly.

I almost lose my balance, and as though Jessie's rooting for me, she gives the halt command.

"Dress center dress!"

Arms up, one hand closed around a fist like we're holding our instruments at attention. Our heads snap to one side, depending on where we are in relation to the fifty-yard line. And that's how we find out there's only two of us left.

We're face-to-face.

Jessie definitely did this on purpose. The part she could do, anyway. I'm a marching star, but I would've been out if she hadn't given the halt command, and this little head-to-head match wouldn't have been possible.

"It's down to Ebony and Josiah, the pride of the brass, trombone versus trumpet, the ultimate face-off."

Our bandmates whistle and swoon because there are no secrets in marching band, and they all know Josiah and I have been circling each other since summer band camp. I'm immediately hot, despite the night, despite the wind, despite that I'm not wearing a jacket or gloves. But we're still at dress, and I can't look away — not that I *want* to look away. I just don't want to be the center of attention while Josiah's adorable, wind-rouged face is staring back at me.

Get it together, Ebbie.

"Atten-HUT!"

We snap our heads front, simultaneously bringing our hands down and back to our sides, chins slightly up.

I am going to win.

For my girls. For my section. For my pride. I am going to beat him and then I'm going to ask him to Homecoming.

Jessie tips her chin, almost too slightly to notice. It's not a cheat. I have no idea what she'll say. It just means she's rooting for me. She loves her little brother, but she was in my section before she was promoted last year, and let's just say that trumps blood. I mean, we've got matching shirts for god's sake.

Trombonists Do It in Seven Positions.

And don't you forget it.

"Mark time!"

The drumline starts up again.

"Backward. March!"

As Josiah and I take off toward the back of the field, eyes and bodies still facing our company, the trumpet section surprises everybody. The school fight song blasts into the open night air, and the rest of the band shrieks and rushes to grab their instruments.

"Slide right," Jessie shouts into the bullhorn. "March!"

Torso front, I twist the bottom half of my body and march toward the home goalposts I can't see.

My trombones are up now, and at first they're pretty terrible. Cold brass doesn't sound so hot. It doesn't matter; they're doing it to cheer me on, waving their bells and slides high, and side to side.

At Jessie's command, Josiah and I march forward, to the rear, and then mark time.

We halt.

We resume, straight from attention, no marking first.

We halt again.

"About-face!"

Right toe behind my left foot, and spin.

"About-face!"

And I'm facing the back of the field again.

"About-face!"

I hate Jessie sometimes.

Between her command, and the band members who abandon the second run-through of the fight song to yell it immediately after her, Josiah and I are spinning like tops.

Even when their laughter becomes contagious, and I can't keep a straight face, and the flute section has inexplicably started playing some super-old-school Taylor Swift song, I keep going. The lights and the empty stands and the brass bells and the friends swirling through my vision.

And then the commands stop, but it's so loud I don't hear what to do next. I legit cannot see anything, my sides are hurting from laughing, and I'm still at attention.

"Ebbie, you won!" Jessie and the rest of the trombones are right there, one of them shaking me by the shoulders.

Josiah's on the ground nearby.

"Did you fall?" I ask with what little breath I have left.

He makes a face and takes his head in his hands.

"Drill down champ!" Jessie shouts, holding one of my hands high. "Homecoming edition!"

"We'll get you a sash to wear next Friday," someone offers.

I did it. And no one can tell I'm on the verge of yarfing on the field.

"Good job, runner-up," I say to Josiah when I offer him my hand, wondering for a moment whether he waited there for me. His section-mates joined him on the ground instead of helping him up, but I wouldn't put it past any of them to be in on it too. This is marching band.

I don't know how cold I am until I'm touching him. He takes my extended hand but keeps his elbow slack so that when he rocks back and hops to his feet, it's on his own strength.

He's just holding my hand.

My ice brick of a hand is slowly warming against Josiah's, and we're all walking back to the stands to collect our backpacks and jackets and instruments. My tongue may as well be a brick too, because now that I'm crowned drill down champ, and we'll all be dispersing, disappearing into the night or mingling in the parking lot while the adrenaline wears off, I don't know what to say. If there was a perfect moment to ask Josiah to the dance, the way I just assumed there would be, I missed it. Now we're at the stands and he's leading me to my stuff before our hands have to separate so he can gather his own.

It turns out I'm not as smooth as I thought.

"Be right back," he says, squeezing my hand before letting go. He does that shy smile I love — the one that tells me I'd really better woman up if I want this to go anywhere — and heads toward his trumpet case.

Come. On. Do better, Ebbie.

And then as usual, Jessie saves the day.

"Ebony, I've gotta take a bunch of kids home," she says, letting her shoulder crash into mine while she slides into her letterman. "Can you do me a favor and give Jo a lift? I'm probably gonna be all night."

"All night? Really?" I'm nodding at friends as they wave goodbye while keeping an eyebrow cocked for Jessie. She's my drum major, but she's also my friend, and she's also my crush's sister who keeps badgering me to "hurry it up" putting the moves on him. Which is only slightly weird.

We've had plenty of opportunities this year alone, as far as she's concerned. Two away competitions since the school year began, which means two bus rides — and marching band travel is hookup heaven. Long road trips on a charter bus with mood lighting and one adult who never seems to make it all the way to the back. And then there's the competition itself. Sure we're changing in front of each other too quickly to care what anyone looks like under their clothes, and then we're rehearsing the music in a tight coil around Jessie, and then we're competing on the field, and then we're marching in front of the judges while the drumline blows everyone away. But between the time we leave the field until the award ceremony starts?

Hook. Up. Heaven.

I mean. If you're so inclined.

Back on the bus or stealing around the hosting campus or at the top of the stands, behind the lights, in the shadows. I don't know how spectators and parents aren't just constantly stumbling onto kids making out. It really wouldn't be hard.

But Josiah and I haven't even kissed, and not for lack of me daydreaming about it. Even sometimes while warming up. We're both brass players, with precision embouchure control. (It's all in the mouth muscles, right?)

Now Jessie's getting impatient. Everyone is. We're getting routinely ditched together, no one's leaving room for us at the table when we stop for dinner on the way home from a performance. The people demand action.

"Josiah," I call without answering Jessie, and when he looks up while slinging his backpack over one shoulder, I feel like my eyes bulge out of my sockets, heart-shaped. "You're riding with me."

"Cool."

"Cool," Jessie echoes her brother, and then tips her forehead close to me. "Take your time."

"Shut up," I hiss, trying to quiet the butterflies careening through my stomach.

I wish I had a cool car. I mean, I wish I had my own car, period.

"Sorry I don't have anything good," I say to Josiah while I run through my mom's preset radio stations as though there's even a slim chance of stumbling on something at all acceptable.

"It's okay, really. Whatever you usually listen to."

"I usually don't." When I catch his glance in my peripheral vision, I clarify. "I don't usually listen to the radio or CDs in the car. I try to run through the trombone part on the way to and from school."

"What, in your head?"

I can't tell if he's making fun of me.

"Yeah. Or like, I'll hum it."

He's smiling.

"From start to finish," I continue, smiling too. "It's really embarrassing."

"Why's it embarrassing?"

"Because I don't notice how hard I'm nodding until I get to like a stop sign and early morning commuters are super unamused."

"You're keeping time, though, I get it," he says through a laugh, lying full against the headrest like we carpool all the time, and we're totally comfortable together. "They're just not band geeks." He shrugs. "Their loss."

"Right?" I keep trying to settle my smile, but every time I glance over, he does too, and it starts back up.

For a moment, it's just comfortably quiet. All I hear is the soft purr of my mom's car while we idle at a stoplight. But we're almost to his place and I haven't popped the question. One more light, then a right turn at the gas station, and a couple residential blocks after that.

I should've driven more slowly. Or suggested we stop and grab a bite to eat. Something to give us a little more time together before the night ends.

I don't want it to be over.

I don't want to go home and fall asleep and have to start all over getting close to him tomorrow.

I'm about to do it. I'm about to ask Josiah if he wants to get drive-thru — the Homecoming proposal will just naturally flow out of that, I tell myself — and then there are lights in my rearview.

Red and blue.

I'm cold all over again.

"I think those are for me," I say, and even I can't hear how scared I am.

"Are you sure?" Josiah asks, twisting in the passenger seat to gawk out the back windshield like all he feels is general curiosity. "We weren't going very fast."

Was I going too slow?

Did I forget to use my blinker? But I haven't changed lanes in forever.

Did I swerve when I glanced at Josiah?

Have I looked over too many times?

My hands are at nine and three, white-knuckle tight around the steering wheel.

The gas station is coming up, and I wonder if I'm allowed to pull into the parking lot. I don't know what to do. I don't know what to say to Josiah. I keep almost forgetting he's beside me and then freaking out that he is.

Behind me, the police cruiser lets out a weird *brrp-brrp*, like someone's warming up a brass mouthpiece. Like I don't know it's following me even though I've dramatically reduced my speed.

"Everything's okay," I say to Josiah, but I'm biting my lip. He doesn't respond, but I say it one more time as I pull under the gas station canopy.

The cruiser pulls in behind me and we park by the station where you buy air for your tires.

"Turn off your engine."

The command blares out over an intercom and my heart jumps three feet.

Oh God. Please please please.

I turn the key in the ignition.

Everything's okay. Be calm. Be polite. Be calm.

Josiah puts his hand on mine, and I remember again that he's there.

I want to tell him we shouldn't move too much but I don't. I don't want him to know how afraid I am. I don't want him to know why this would scare me. I want to go back in time, rewind all the way back to the stadium, to the lights, to the field. I don't want to be Ebony, an anonymous Black girl in her mom's car, joyriding in the middle of a school night; I want to be Ebony, drill down champ, first chair trombone, section leader. I want to be with my bandmates, surrounded. Safe.

But Josiah's here. His hand is squeezing mine, and he's totally calm.

Maybe it's a good thing.

Maybe I won't be a hashtag.

Maybe no one will have to remind people to say my name.

Maybe it's a good thing there's a white kid in the car with me. I can't remember a single story of a Black woman or man or kid being shot when they had a white passenger.

Maybe this is like a band inspection. We pass or fail together.

My hand's sweating and Josiah must have noticed by now, but I don't let go until the officer makes it to my window and motions for me to put it down.

I fumble for a moment, let go of Josiah in case I need to get the registration from the glove compartment, remember I haven't lowered the window yet, and reach over to do it before remembering I could've used my left hand.

The officer knocks on my window again, just as it starts to glide down. The night air gets in.

"Good evening, miss."

"Hi," I blurt. I want to point to my passenger and make sure the officer sees that he's there, that I'm not alone. I don't have my phone out, I'm not livestreaming the way I swore I would be if I ever got pulled over or detained or confronted by the liaison officer at our school, but I'm not alone. Josiah's with me, so nothing bad can happen.

But this is real life. This is happening to me, the way it was never supposed to.

Nothing's happening. You're gonna get a ticket and Mom'll take her keys for a little while.

Nothing is happening.

So why can't I breathe?

Because he's standing next to me. His crisp blue uniform is filling up my window; it's all I can see, even though I'm still facing my steering wheel.

Slide right.

"Do you know why I pulled you over?"

Dress left.

My head snaps to face him, so I can say no. I don't know why this is happening — but he doesn't tell me.

"License and registration. Proof of insurance."

My fingers refuse not to fumble, but I deliver what he's asking for and then cradle my hands in my lap.

"Where are you going?"

I dress left again, feel my mouth gape before the words fall free.

"We had practice," I blurt. "Marching band."

"Marching band practice," he repeats while he shuffles through my documents. "At night? What do you play?"

"It's when the football field is free," I say, but I don't know if that's true. I didn't invent band practice; nobody conferred with me before making the schedule. I shake my head to keep it clear. "Trombone. I play trombone; my friend plays trumpet."

"Seems late." The officer hands back my things. Maybe this is almost over. Maybe I'm anxious over nothing, and silly for being afraid.

Sandra Bland.

I jolt in my seat.

As you were.

As you were. As you were.

"Homecoming's next weekend," I say, and my voice croaks around the lump in my throat. I wish I could see my mother, and then the desire itself makes me want to cry. "Our director added a new closer."

"Closer."

"The last song in the field show. He added a new one. For halftime at the Homecoming game. We had to learn it."

I glance over at Josiah for corroboration, but he just gives a little smile like I'm chatting with a friend while he patiently waits.

Dress —

"Well, Ebony, that doesn't tell me where you're going."

For a moment I don't understand how the policeman knows my name. Or I don't like that he does. It feels like he's nearer now, but he isn't. It feels like he's larger, but he's not. I just want to go.

"Home. I'm going home."

He finally leans down to peer into the car.

"You two live together?"

"No, sir," Josiah says through an easy laugh.

"A little young for that, I guess," the cop replies, before standing.

I can breathe again.

"Step out of the car, Ebony." He says it like it's a question. But I can't.

I can't.

I'm at attention. My joints are locked, and I am solid rock.

He wants me to get out but I don't know how to move. I don't know how to make myself open the door, but I have to.

At rest.

"Ebony? Out of the car, please."

And I find myself being grateful for his patience. I'm lucky he hasn't taken my shakiness for resistance, that he hasn't taken anything from his holster. I've seen videos of people being tased, the way they seize up and convulse. The way they look terrified and the way they go quiet even when they want to scream. I've seen the kind of bruises rubber bullets make, and the way a girl exactly my size is easily body-slammed, or wrestled to the ground when she's dressed for a pool party.

He's a good cop, I tell myself so I can open my car door without asking him why. *He's one of the good ones.*

We're still at the gas station, just beyond the canopy pouring harsh light over the rows of pumps and concrete.

The light is so different than on the field. The autumn air too. It isn't crisp; it's cutting.

There's electricity, but it's not the same.

There are no stands, but there's an audience. People rubbernecking as they walk past us on their way to the shop, or pretending not to stare while they fill their tanks.

"Step this way, please," the officer says, and for the first time I realize he has a partner. She's standing on the passenger side of my mom's car, next to Josiah — who's still inside.

Good. I hope they let him be. I hope this doesn't get any more embarrassing than it already is. I hope because of him, they let us go soon.

"Is something wrong?" I manage to ask the first cop when we're a few steps away. I even try to smile.

"You seem really anxious, Ebony," he tells me. "And part of my training as an officer is to recognize those cues."

I feel stupid smiling and nodding, but I don't know what else to do.

"So I'm gonna ask you to submit to a search of your person and your vehicle so that we're satisfied you're not hiding anything from us. If everything checks out, you can go on your way. How does that sound?"

Halt!

Halt!

"Mhm." I nod enthusiastically.

The cutting breeze tightens the skin on my face in

two distinct stripes, drying tears that must have streaked my cheeks without my noticing. If the officer sees them, he doesn't say anything, and without him asking me to, I get down on my knees because that's what I remember a policeman saying someone should've done to avoid being manhandled or choked.

I hear gravel crunch under my jeans, but I don't feel it. I'm losing senses, and I don't know how to stop it. It isn't safe. I have to know what's going on, to pay attention, to hear the commands when they come so I don't make a wrong move. But my brain is turning off. Not the way it does when the routine's memorized and muscle memory will carry me through. It's turning off the way it does when I'm listening to the news say a twelve-year-old shouldn't have been playing in a park, as if that's the reason the child is dead.

Atten-hut!

I am kneeling on the ground in the middle of the night, in a parking lot filling up with people if the now abundant footfalls are any indication, and I am near but not beneath the lights.

The football field is a million years ago. I can hear the music somewhere far away. My music, my trombone section, off in the distance. The alternate song we've had memorized since the middle of the summer, that we just put to steps tonight. The dramatic twelve counts the brass marches at half-tempo, while the high winds cover more ground, fanning out while we seem to move in slow motion. The way my heart swelled in my chest.

"Go ahead and lay flat," the officer tells me, and I hear myself sob while hot tears slide. They slap the pavement next to me when I'm on my stomach.

Why is this happening? What did I do wrong?

Nothing. Everything's okay.

But it can't be, otherwise why am I on the ground?

Hands pat my sides, starting at my rib cage, wrapping around to momentarily grip my front pockets before checking the ones at the back of my jeans. Two fingers slide into my back pocket and I know what they pull out.

My count sheet.

A small rectangle of paper, with five columns and a dozen rows.

Set.

Move.

Count.

Side to side.

Front to back.

Everything I need to know to find my position on the field, and how to get from one to the next. Everything I need to be part of a breathtaking portrait that comes to life when the music starts.

Almost everything.

I also need to see where the rest of my company stands. I need them on the field with me. I need to find my designated spot, and then adjust my position to fit neatly into the design we're making together. That's the only way to know I'm right.

That's the beauty of marching band. The collective trumps everything, including the coordinates. We dress to each other, and then — *then* — I know where I am, and where I'm meant to be.

It's still true, I tell myself. *Josiah's in the car.*

I'm not alone.

Then the officer pats the inside of my legs. I gasp and he hesitates, because he felt it too. The cold wetness that bled through the denim when he pressed my jeans against my skin.

I don't know when it happened, but at least I didn't pee a lot.

It's just a tiny bit.

I hadn't even noticed, but now we both know. . . .

There's no command for this. There's no way to wipe it clean. There's no magic phrase that will undo all of this, or make it beautiful.

My shoulders go slack, and when I let my forehead rest against the pavement, my breath leaves in a long, low moan. The timbre is flat, like an instrument out of tune.

I wish none of this had happened, and I wish it was done.

The officer helps me to my feet, and when I look at him, I'm crying all over again. But he looks changed too. He's not stoic or certain now, and I'm not imagining it. I know because his hand's still on my elbow but it's keeping me upright.

Maybe all I had to do was piss myself to save my life. To turn a grip into a cradle. Maybe all the Black girls I've seen brutalized on camera and then blamed for their own abuse just didn't make themselves pathetic enough.

I'm champ twice in the same, awful night.

But the electricity's still there, behind me. There's something nipping in the air. The policeman's lips part but he doesn't speak. I'll have to turn around and see for myself.

I KNEW YOU WERE 𝄞 WHEN YOU WALKED IN . . .

Except instead of spelling out "trouble," he's drawn a treble clef.

Josiah.

He's out of the car, holding a sign.

I KNEW YOU WERE TREBLE WHEN YOU WALKED IN . . . He's looking down at the poster board like he's reading it along with me. Like he's admiring all the musical symbols and all the glitter too. Like we're passing notes in the hall and trying to make each other laugh with bad band puns.

But he's not alone; everyone's here.

Our bandmates. All the footfalls I heard when I was facedown on the concrete, with the smell of gasoline flooding my nostrils like there was an invisible oil spill — they were them. Because they knew all along. In my head, I hear the flutes play the song the way they did during the drill down.

Jessie's beaming at me, and my heart sinks.

A dozen phones are pointed at me. They're recording this.

Whatever this is.

"Ebony," Josiah says. "Will you go to Homecoming with me?"

And then they're cheering.

Josiah's trumpet section has horns out again. They're blasting pep band riffs into the night air, attracting even more attention in the lot of the too-bright gas station — but it sounds off. Like those charmless horns people blare at soccer games. It doesn't sound right.

None of this is right.

"Surprise!" Jessie erupts, like maybe that'll help me understand. She's bouncing up and down, despite the camera she's got trained on me. She's contorting her mouth in a mock scream, pantomiming excitement and disbelief in the hopes that I'll catch on. "It's a promposal! Well, a Homecoming-posal!"

And they all laugh. Because this is a setup.

None of this was real. Except the damp spot in the crotch of my jeans. . . .

I look left at the shamefaced police officer, then forward to see Josiah, whose smile is soft but excited.

Dress center.

There's nothing to be afraid of.

It was all for Homecoming.

"This is why you wanted a ride," I say, and it sounds so atonal, it could be a question or an accusation. "No, Jessie —"

"It was all Josiah," she blurts, still beaming. "I was just following orders."

"For once," someone says, and everyone laughs.

The whole world laughs.

It's funny because she's our drum major. She *gives* orders; we take them. We're her marching band.

I study the faces surrounding Josiah's.

This is my marching band. This is my company.

You wanted to ask him to the dance, Ebbie.

This is what you wanted.

But the inside of my right pant leg is wet.

The skin on both my knees is dimpled.

There's chalky dust on my band shirt from lying on the ground, and probably on my forehead too.

"Ebbie." Josiah says my name and my chin snaps up like I've been called to attention.

They're all waiting.

This is the part where I get in line. Where I adjust my position. Where I dress right and left and center, so we're all in sync. So we're all in this together. So we're one.

We pass or fail as a unit.

"Ebbie?"

Dress center dress.

Only, something stops me. The same thing that makes my breath come fast and hard. That makes the police officer slowly take back his hand and shift his weight away.

Don't make a scene. Don't overreact.

But those commands aren't from a drum major; they're the ones I knew before marching band. Before high school. Before junior high. Maybe I've known them from birth.

Don't get angry. Don't make them feel bad. Don't cross your arms or ball your fists or grit your teeth.

They didn't know.

"Eb?" Josiah's smile is fading at last.

Dress center —

I reject this inspection. I break rank, allow myself to shake my head, to furrow my brow even though they're all so happy. I keep my eyes trained on Josiah so that he's the first to know.

This is not okay.

"No," I say.

It goes very quiet. The band and the little crowd that's joined us all stop. Now I can hear the cars passing on the street and the chime when someone goes into the gas station shop. Now it's easier to tell we're not on the field, or at a competition, and that here there are several sets of lights, and one of them is blue and red.

We're not a company here; we can't be. I'm the only one crying.

"No," I say again, even though they're still recording. Even though they heard me the first time. "I won't go to Homecoming with you."

When I move toward my mom's car, I'm the only one who does.

"Why not?" Josiah asks, the sign still in both hands.

"Because," I tell him, before I climb back in. "You don't know how horrible this is."

Maybe the wind picked up again and appled his cheeks, or maybe he did that on his own. Either way, Josiah's brow is furrowed now, but he's too many steps behind.

"As you were," I tell him, and then the shamefaced officer opens my car door for me so that I can drive myself home.

THE REAL ONES

BY SOFIA QUINTERO

12:28 A.M.

@Jordan-Caceres Bruh, let me tell u how u no u got a real one. When it comes to ur ex, she dont be pressed but she aint about to let sum chick be out here talkin slick about u either. She realizes that u chose her and stands by u no matter what. And if that mean she got to check a bih, she gonna handle it. @Camila-Rose-Olivo is the realist girl u can find but back up fore u catch these paws cuz she mine lol!!!

12:31 a.m.

u c wut I posted on IG with the pic of us at the carnival I took u last wknd?

Yeah. That was nice.

Nice? Dassit? Wow lol

I luv that pic of us. And that was sweet wut u wrote. Thank u.

u aint even like it or comment or anything!

I just liked it now.

u need to send it 2 Kateleen. And tag me.

12:48 a.m.

Wow.

OK I c u

Wut u want from me Jordan???

I claimed u Cami!!! Thats wut u been wantin right???

Yeah. And now u want me to fight Kateleen 2moro. So we good right?

12:56 a.m.

Jordan?

I don't want to fight with u too.

Neither do I. Its late so Imma fall out.
TTYL.

7:53 A.M.

Cami regretted telling Titi Steph about the fight even though she gave her aunt a dique hypothetical. Made it seem like it was a random girl at school who was squaring up with her former best friend to prove that she was a real one. Now Titi Steph was on a tear about how different things were Back in the Day. Cami used to love when Mami and Titi Steph got going about Back in the Day, especially when they talked about slang, broke out Polaroids to show Cami the clothes, and, most of all, when they played the music. With Mami gone and Titi Steph on her own, however, talks about Back in the Day always led to lectures about how "y'all kids these days" were failing.

"Nena, lemme tell you," said Titi Steph as she pulled off the Major Deegan toward the school. "I couldn't be a teenager today. When we was coming up, you had beef with a girl — that's what we called it. Do y'all still call it that?" Cami just rubbed a smudge on her window. "Or static. Sometimes we called it static. But anyway, when we had static with another girl, and it got to the point we were gonna fight, we had a fair fight y ya se acabó." Titi stopped for a light, the break allowing her hands to get in on her spiel. "And y'all kids jumping people now. Where y'all get that from?"

When Titi Steph launched this rant, Cami decided to fix her mistake of telling her about two girls planning to fight after school by biting her tongue. But now she had to say something. "I dunno!" She had never jumped anyone, would never jump anyone, and sure as hell didn't want to get jumped! "Maybe from whoever's raising us."

¿Pa' que fue eso? It just put a battery in Titi's back. "Nuh-uh, y'all ain't get that from us. . . ."

"When you had to fight, you didn't bring your girls?" Cami didn't want Savannah and Jewel to jump Kateleen, but she knew she could count on them to be at the Harris Park ball field at three o'clock in case Kateleen's friends went by a different code. Truth was, Cami didn't want to show up herself. Mami would have seen right through her hypothetical, started asking a million questions, insisted on picking up Cami after school. But she should've known better than to expect Titi Steph to give Cami that out, inadvertently or not.

"Whenever we was gonna fight, yeah, we all brought our girls. But that was to keep the fight fair. Not to jump somebody." Titi Steph slapped the steering wheel as punctuation. "Your generation, y'all be metiendose in the drama, escalating things and calling that loyalty."

Cami shrugged and waited for Titi to go in on social media. And five, four, three . . .

"Back in the Day, we had a fair fight, and no one jumped in until blood was drawn. *That's* when your girls jumped in to break it up, 'fore anybody got seriously hurt. We broke it up and went home." The light turned green, and Titi drove. "Honestly, Cami, I actually feel bad for y'all. Y'all never get a break. Con el Facebook y Instagram y Chatsnack . . ."

"It's Snapchat, Titi."

"Snatchchat?!?"

"SNAP . . . chAT. Don't worry about it, Titi. Snapchat been dead."

"Anyway, Back in the Day, you had a fair fight on Friday, cooled off over the weekend, and on Monday everybody came to school like nothing happened. That was the end of it. Pero ustedes tiene toda esa social media and . . . and the instigators! Don't get me wrong. Back in the Day, we had instigators too. Like we had this girl named Cindy. Always bochinchando and stirring the pot, freakin' Cindy. But we *ain't* like kids like that." For a fleeting second, Titi's nostalgic smile betrayed her words. "You did not want to be known as an instigator. Maybe we weren't mature enough to ignore them, but we had the sense not to trust 'em, ya know. But today you kids don't get to cool off. You got a hundred instigators fanning the flames on Facebook or whatever wanting to see two girls try to kill each other."

Titi made a slow turn onto the school's block, and Cami's belly stretched tight. Her cell phone burned in her back pocket with forty-plus Instagram notifications and counting. Most of the comments were anti-Kateleen, but that just made Cami feel worse.

Only one post didn't encourage the fight — a girl Cami didn't even know but who clearly remembered them from middle school. *Maybe it's just me but this makes me kinda sad. You two used to be so tight. Your friend-ship was #goals. Over a boy too? SMH.* And just like Titi Steph said, it took seconds before people swarmed the girl's comment with replies ordering her to STFU, calling her out her name and telling her to mind her business as if any of them were minding theirs. Cami wanted to DM her, but she soon deleted her comment, leaving all the hate marooned on Jordan's page.

As per their ritual, Cami planted a kiss on Titi's cheek and opened the car door. She had one foot on the curb when Titi said, "I mean, you girls got a lot to be angry about. And it's the same thing. Why take it out on each other?" Hopelessness smoothed out the usual gravel in Titi's voice, and Cami twisted back to throw her arms around her aunt's neck. Then she darted out the car and into the school building.

9:03 A.M.

The three minutes between first and second period were never enough time.

As he walked Cami to her next class, Jordan asked, "Where were you this morning?" He reached for her arm.

"Late." Cami wriggled from his grip. Jordan insisted she come to school early so they could "hang out" in stairwell E, but he was always late. When he showed up, they talked about whatever was poppin' on Netflix for two minutes and then made out for ten grabby more until the first bell. "For once *I* was late, K."

"I'm not mad or anything." Cami kept her eyes on the floor tiles before her even as Jordan slung his arm around her shoulder. She used to keep her head up, basking in those three minutes of having her arm hooked through his as Jordan gave high fives and upnods to his boys in the corridors. Today though, if she looked up, looked at him, saw their classmates whispering about the upcoming fight, she might scream, and that could only make things worse. Jordan said, "We good. So long as you not late after school and have me out here looking crazy."

Cami halted and made herself face him. "Make *you* look crazy?"

"What you want me to do, Cami?" Jordan scoffed, exasperated that he had to explain something so basic to her. "Kateleen out here wildin', calling me trash and whatnot, and what I'm supposed to do? Fight a female? You my girl, right?"

The bell rang just as they arrived at Cami's classroom, and other kids bustled by them into the lab. As her teacher strode toward the door, Cami finally said, "You asking me?"

She slipped into the classroom and toward her station, fighting the urge to turn around even though she wanted to watch the teacher close the door on Jordan. Would he crack his joke of the day and make everyone laugh? How long would Jordan stand there and wait for Cami to steal one last look at him? Would he blow her a kiss or mouth *Text me*?

Why did she care?

Three minutes was way too much time.

10:28 A.M.

Kateleen's new ride or die Lisanne had started taunting Cami in the locker room. *I feel like somebody's getting they ass whooped today,* she sang over the lockers several rows away with a chorus of giggles accompanying her. *I wonder who it is. Is it you, you, you, you, you?*

"Let me go over there real quick," said Cami's friend Savannah. She twisted her long hair into a loose bun on her head and slammed her locker door shut.

"No," said their other friend Jewel. "If they really want it, let them start it."

Kateleen usually cut third-period gym, but now she stood on the opposite side of the volleyball net, scowling at Cami through the nylon. Ignoring their oblivious gym teacher's instructions, Jewel yelled, "Cami, let's switch." Without another word, they swapped places so Cami could play libero even though she had a killer spike. With Savannah on the same team as Kateleen and on the opposite side of the zone, Cami believed they would get through gym on what Titi Steph called *Don't start none, won't be none.*

And then Jewel spiked the ball into a gap that Savannah and Kateleen raced to close. They collided, the ball bouncing off the knot of their bodies. The gym teacher blew her whistle, and many of their classmates laughed at the spontaneous slapstick with Lisanne's cackle blasting to the rafters.

In the same instant, Savannah caught her breath and spun on her heel. "What's so freakin' funny?" Before Lisanne could answer, she rocketed toward her. The two girls began windmilling for the other's hair, creating a vortex that sucked in all their classmates as they attempted to stop the pending fight.

Cami dove into the scrum and frantically grasped for Savannah amidst the competing limbs. Through the field of flailing arms, she saw Kateleen grab a fistful of Lisanne's T-shirt and haul her backward. Just as Cami got ahold of Savannah, she and Kateleen caught eyes. Cami realized too late that Kateleen was within scratching distance. Refusing to let Savannah go yet also needing to protect herself, Cami reared her head as far as she could, shut her eyes, and waited for the sting of Kateleen's nails digging into her cheek.

Instead she felt the tension in her outstretched arms go slack. Cami opened her eyes and found herself in the outer ring of a smaller cluster of girls pulling Savannah toward the locker room. Like a cell split during mitosis, the other truss of girls pushed Lisanne toward the bleachers as she cursed over Kateleen's head despite her friend's repeated pleas to chill.

As their classmates widened the gap between Savannah and Lisanne, Cami found herself wanting Kateleen to look at her again. Almost as if she had called her name, Kateleen looked over her shoulder, and they caught eye once again. In that second, Cami saw something she recognized. Something she missed. Trusted.

Sometimes fifty minutes was not enough.

Heard yall already got it poppin. Thats wuts up! THATS MY GURL!!!

11:58 A.M.

"Yo, you got to hit her first," said Savannah. She dropped her backpack on the bench and balled her fist. "While she running her mouth just go POP!" Savannah punched the air, and Cami's face flushed knowing that Kateleen and her friends were glaring at them across the cafeteria.

"Sit down," said Cami. "Please." Mami said striking the first blow was always wrong no matter what the other person did. Even if they called you out your name, talked about your mama, or got in your face, you only struck in self-defense. Cami remembered Mami and Titi Steph sharing a high five with Titi Steph adding, *You don't start it, but you finish it!* Kateleen had a shot at Cami but kept it old-school.

"What? You afraid of her?" Savannah started bouncing like a boxer in her corner. "'Cause I'm not afraid of no-freakin'-body."

"We know, S'vannah." Jewel cut the pool of ketchup in her Styrofoam tray with a wilting French fry. "Sit down already. You making me dizzy."

Savannah dropped onto the bench. "I'm just sayin', Cami. I got your back. Nobody gonna jump you on my watch 'cause I'm loyal AF."

Cami mumbled thanks, her gratitude matching Savannah's comfort.

Jewel asked, "Are you really going to fight her though?"

"What kinda question is that?" Savannah yelled. "That ho coming after her man."

"Even if she were chasing Jordan like he says, why does Cami have to say anything never mind put her hands on her?" said Jewel. "Let him tell Kateleen to back off."

Savannah rolled her eyes. "Nobody can make someone respect you but you."

"Way I see it . . ." Jewel stole a glance at Cami through the corner of her oversized frames. ". . . Jordan the one being disrespectful."

Savannah gasped. "How you figure?" Instead of waiting for Jewel's explanation, Cami picked up her backpack and walked toward the exit. "Camila!" Savannah called, but she refused to turn around. Even when Lisanne tossed her milk carton at her.

1:22 P.M.

Cami asked Ms. Campbell for a pass to get a drink of water. At the fountain, she looked around her before pulling out her cell phone.

Baby, you need me to pick you up from school today?

If you want me to get you, let me know before two.

I got a customer coming in for his inspection at three but I can get another mechanic to take care of him if I have to get to you.

Camila Rose you better stay away from that fight!!!

Cami was unsure whether her aunt believed her to be inocente or had figured out she was the one planning to fight, but she was confident that was on purpose. Another way Titi Steph was different than Mami. She would wait for Cami to explicitly ask for her help even if that was the last thing Cami wanted her to do. Cami texted, *Yeah pick me up today.* She couldn't prevent the fight by letting Titi Steph know about it, but if it did go down, she wanted it to be cut short by the car turning the corner to whisk her away.

Then she made the mistake of checking her notifications. Word spread about what happened in gym, sparking thirty-eight additional flame-fanning comments. Cami scanned the thread looking for a comment from Kateleen. The Kateleen she remembered would have read every word. The Kateleen who would have lunged at her third period and wouldn't have let a single post stand without comment said nothing. Not a single clapback since Jordan's early morning post.

Cami considered all the possible outcomes of the text she had been composing in her head since third period. She had nothing to lose. Kateleen might try to set her up — like pretend they were cool only to turn on her once she had an audience — but Titi Steph taught Cami to watch her back. Kateleen might read Cami for filth, but how low would she go knowing Cami knew things about Kateleen that she didn't want anyone else to know? Cami had no intention of saying anything that could embarrass her should Kateleen screencap her texts and forward them to the world.

Really the worst thing that could happen was Kateleen not responding to Cami at all. Ignoring Cami would bind her guts in a twist for another ninety-one minutes until the final bell rang, and everyone rushed out the door to Harris Park for the fight. That she could not stomach. . . .

1:26 p.m.

Hi Kate

If u make me I will but I dont really want to fight u tbqh

I dont think its right for girls to be fighting over no guy so if u really really want Jordan u can have him

I DONT WANT HIS ASS!!!

LOL

So we still got things in common 8^p

Im surprised u still got my number in ur phone.

Yeah I never deleted it.

I guess I was kinda hopin we would find some way to be friends again at one point. And if u dont ever want that I can respect that. But like I said that dont mean I want static with u

Static? Wut does that mean?

Problems trouble or whatever. Something my aunt says. It musta stuck lol.

OMG! How is Titi Steph??? Tell her I said hi!!!!!

She good! Got a new girlfriend. Im like I like her but dont be movin her in no time soon lol.

LMAO!!!

Have you seen your dad lately?

> Not tryin to be nosey or anything. U dont gotta answer.

> Nvm

No its OK

They denied his parole.

> Damn I thought for sure they would let him come home once they found out he was sick.

Hes gonna die in there Cami

> Im sorry Katie. I really am. Next time u go up to visit him call me if u need somebody to go with u.

> I mean u were there for me when Mami passed so Ima be there 4 u.

> Only if u want.

"Get off your phone, and back to class, Miss Olivo!"

2:53 P.M.

Cami stepped out of her eighth-period class to find Savannah and Jewel already waiting for her. So were the paparazzi. Some kids already had their cell phones up and recording. Savannah and Jewel hooked their arms through Cami's and steered her across the crowded hallway and into the girls' room. A few busybodies attempted to follow them, but Savannah shooed them off and threw her weight behind the door. "What's the plan?" she asked over the pounding on the door by the gossip zombies.

"I texted Kateleen." Without mentioning Kateleen's dad, Cami summarized their exchange. "She says she doesn't want to fight."

"Lemme see," said Savannah, demanding Cami's cell phone.

"No." Even though Savannah and Jewel were her best friends now, Cami could not betray Kateleen's confidence. Nor was she ready to admit to them that she initiated contact in an attempt to avoid the fight.

"Why?"

Jewel raised her hands, motioning for them to stop. "You all don't need to be doing this right now." She turned to Cami. "You sure she's just not trying to set you up?"

"No." Cami inhaled. "Does that really matter?"

"What do you want us to do, Cam?" asked Jewel. "How do we have your back?"

Cami pulled out her cell phone. Ignoring the now eighty-nine notifications on Jordan's post, she found an old post of herself with Kateleen blowing kisses at the camera while on a field trip to the Botanical Garden. The girls had posed before a burst of orchids dancing above their heads like a halo of fuchsia butterflies. The caption was Kateleen's suggestion: *#Whoneedsfilterswhenyougottherealthing.* So many of the classmates who had hearted the photo and wrote comments like *#friendshipgoals* had now taken sides in the fight over Jordan.

Savannah folded her arms across her chest as they waited for Cami to answer. She reposted the photo, tagged all their mutual friends including Jordan, and typed out a new post. Then Cami finally relinquished her phone to Savannah and Jewel. "If you want to have my back, like this. Share it. Comment on it."

Her friends huddled together and hunched over Cami's phone. As Jewel read her new post, a smile grew across her face.

Gurl, let me tell u how u no u got a real one. When people say she the pretty one n u the smart one, she tell em to STFU because u both lit and thats why u besties. She dont let you walk around with cilantro in your teeth, change her password on Netflix, or put all your secrets on IG just cuz u had a disagreement. After ur mama dies she sleeps on ur hard ass floor for a week so when u wake up in the middle of the night crying for your mother she can stroke ur hair and hold ur hand. Even though she mad at me right now @Kateleen-Santos was a real one. A real friend. No matter what happens at the park today, I'm never going to forget that or not appreciate it. And tbh Im not happy that we gonna fight at all never mind over some guy whos probably playin us both! LET'S KEEP IT A BUCK OK!!! Now I dont really believe everybody gotta like each other fr fr. I don have to like u to still want u to win. Disrespect for one girl today means any girl can get it tomorrow. Don't sleep!!! But the girls in this school should put our issues aside to agree on one thing and that's if any dude who called any one of us out our name, we would ALL SHUT HIM DOWN. What if any boy who tried to grope us on the stairwell or play us against each other, every single girl gave him fifty feet? How about if the next time some guy won't use Deidre's pronouns or tells JC to put on a dress, one of the other girls he does want to get with refused to give him any play? Because it really don't matter if we're friends or if we don't like each other. THIS WHOLE SCHOOL WOULD CHANGE FOR THE BETTER FOR ALL OF US!!!

"I got you," said Jewel, reaching for her own cell phone. She found Cami's post on IG and her thumbs flurried across her screen as she typed a reply. "Done."

Cami checked her own phone again. Jewel's response came after a dozen others, the first from Lisanne: *Oh, so now you don't have the same energy you had when trashing @Kateleen-Santos behind her back to @Jordan-Caceres. Scared much? YOU STILL GON CATCH THESE HANDS!!!* But Deidre replied with several hashtags, *#GirlsLikeUs #StickTogether #CISter #ShutHimDown*, and already garnered nineteen likes and a string of affirming memes from *RuPaul's Drag Race* and *Pose*.

Jewel's response, too, already racked up a dozen likes. *I cosign all of this! It's time for girls to quit the #PickMePatrol. Comment if you agree.* The hearts increased while Cami was reading it and then came the first reply.

And where my fellas at? U a #Prove2Me or nah? Holla if u dont need to fix urself by breakin other people.

Cami looked up and gave Savannah the biggest grin. "That post was everything."

Savannah shrugged. "We girls gotta know who we can trust." Then she raised her hands and crossed her fingers. "And if 'Lijah don't comment, I swear, I'ma just start talking to another guy who does." Her phone pinged, and Savannah checked her screen. She belted out a Cardi B cackle. "Come through, Elijah! I knew he would." She showed Cami and Jewel the Boomerang video of him and two of his friends yelling, "HOLLA!"

Jewel laughed and gave Savannah a high five. Then both girls turned to Cami and waited for her guidance. Cami stuffed her phone into her pocket, then made her way to the door. "Let's do this." Savannah and Jewel again hooked their arms through Cami's and ushered her out the bathroom and through the waiting throng.

3:04 P.M.

On their way to Harris Park, some kids egged on the fight. A boy leapt in front of Cami and shoved his cell phone in her face. "Camila, you ready to rock Kateleen's world?"

Savannah clamped her hand over his phone and flung his arm away from Cami. "Cut it out, Corny Levin!"

The crowd cackled at her quip and teased him the rest of the way to the park. Another group had already assembled around the pitcher's mound. Cami searched the faces and found Kateleen studying her phone while circled by her friends, Lisanne yammering in her ear.

Someone spotted Cami approaching. "She here! She ain't skip. She here, yo!" The knot in her belly swelled as she made her way to the mound, and the gawkers clamored for the fight. Kateleen looked up and said something to Cami she could not hear above the crowd.

"What?" Kateleen repeated herself, but Cami still could not make out her words. "Sorry, what?"

"EVERYBODY, SHUT UP!" yelled Savannah. The crowd reduced itself to titters, anticipating the verbal shots that religiously preceded the swinging limbs. Cell phones rose.

Kateleen said, "I said this dude not here, and he not coming."

It took a second for Cami to understand. Jordan? "How do you know?" asked Cami.

Kateleen waved her phone. "See for yourself."

Everyone mimicked Cami as she checked Jordan's IG. His early morning post had disappeared. Savannah and Jewel perched themselves at her shoulders. "What's going on?"

"I'm not sure." Jordan hadn't blocked her from his page, but they were no longer friends. Yet she found a request to be added from Kateleen. Cami smiled and accepted it. She looked up in time to catch Kateleen's smile. She messaged Kateleen through the app.

Need a ride home?

OMG yes. I need to get away from these people. They been on all me all day and IM DONE!!!

Kateleen walked toward Cami, and the crowd gasped. "Here we go, here we go, here we go!!!" With clenched fists, Savannah took a step toward Kateleen, but Jewel quietly blocked her path. Kateleen pulled her arm through Cami's, and they headed out the park. Confusion faded quickly, leaving a trail of boos peppered with a few claps and cheers.

3:12 P.M.

Cami and her three friends found Titi Steph's car and piled giggling into the back seat. "Kateleen!" said Titi Steph. "Long time, no see!"

"I know, right?"

"It's good to see you again, mama."

"It's good to see you too, Titi."

"OK but why alla you gotta cram yourself in the back seat like I'm some kind of chauffeur? Back in the Day we ain't had no Lyft or Uber or nothing like that. Shoo, you think a butch like me could even hail a cab? Ni lo piensa."

Cami smiled at her friends as they prodded Titi Steph to tell them more about Back in the Day. When they got home, she'd fix them some snacks and ask them to help her turn her post into a pledge that anyone who was down with respect could sign. Mami would be so proud.

PARKER OUTSIDE THE BOX

BY RAY STOEVE

THE MESSENGER COMES FOR ME near the end of fourth period, which is perfect, because I'm already hangry. I gather my stuff and follow her, wondering if I can make this quick and get to lunch early.

"Parker!" Ms. Kerry smiles when I walk into her tiny office.

I nod, sitting in one of the chairs in front of her desk. "My grades are up," I say.

"Yes! Yes, they are. That's not why you're here." She folds her hands. "So. You're back up to Bs and Cs, which is great."

I weave my fingers together, cracking my knuckles.

"But there's one thing left before you're set." She shuffles through some papers and hands one to me. I scan the list: the YMCA, the Humane Society, the zoo. "Your community service hours. You have to complete sixty to graduate, and you have five weeks left."

When I walk in the door that afternoon, Kevin is on the couch playing *Call of Duty.* Eric is watching him, because Mom says he's too young to actually play shooter games. I don't know how seeing it is different from doing it, but whatever.

Kevin and Eric are my stepbrothers. Their dad, David, and my mom met when I was in middle school. My parents had just finalized their divorce, and she was looking around on a dating site. David caught her eye: two young kids, recently widowed, with his own veterinary practice. She thought they'd have a lot to talk about, and she was right. Sometimes people stare at us when we're out in public, because Mom and I are white, and David, Kevin, and Eric are Black. But I just glare back, and people usually have the grace to look away.

In my room, I look at the list of organizations. I'm not stoked about this. It was hard enough to get my grades where they were supposed to be. Trying to be a cis girl up until last year tanked my will to do anything else. And now this? In five weeks?

"These are just options," Ms. Kerry had said. "Feel free to find your own."

Sure.

Some of the names on the list are familiar, some aren't. One has "Pride" in the name, so it must be gay-related. The Northwest Pride Association Youth4Youth program. Sounds like an unfortunately named dating site for teenagers.

I ask Siri and she pulls up the website on my phone. It's a local mentorship program based in Seattle and the surrounding area. LGBTQ high school students get paired with younger LGBTQ buddies. Like Big Brothers Big Sisters except I wouldn't have to pick a gender box. That's cool.

Kevin screams the F-word from the living room. Eric's cackle follows. It might not be too bad, hanging out with a kid a few times a week. No worse than my brothers. Especially if all the kid wants to do is shoot hoops and play virtual soldiers.

"I'll do this one," I say, pointing to the mentorship program.

"Wonderful." Ms. Kerry beams at me, and grabs a form from the huge organizer behind her desk. Northwest Pride's logo rainbows across the top.

Name: Parker Johnson

Date of birth: August 10, 2001

Gender:

There's more than two boxes. There's male, female, nonbinary, even a fill in the blank. I've never seen a form with these options before. I check off "nonbinary," and it feels like letting out a breath I've been holding for years.

Ms. Kerry is still smiling at me when I hand back the form, the kind of smile cis people give when they're all excited to witness me being my True Self. "I'll send this over and they'll get in touch with you soon."

"Cool." I escape the office and head for class.

I came out as nonbinary at the beginning of last year, but some people (cough adults cough) still act like it was yesterday, like this is something new and adorable. Or new and confusing. My friends don't give a shit; they switched pronouns without a blink. My family was just glad they didn't have to use a new name.

I'm pretty happy the way I am, but sometimes I think I should do something more. You know, march in a protest, change the way I look. Some people bind, but not me. Not because I don't want to. But binders are too tight, and too warm, and turn my shoulder muscles into what feels like pincushions for invisible, white-hot needles. So yeah. People see my long hair and my chest and think girl. But everyone who matters just sees me. That's how I want it. I shouldn't have to cut my hair and flatten my chest and shrink to a size six just to be taken seriously.

Family dinner night is Friday, the only day Mom doesn't work the evening shift at the hospital. David has Kevin in the kitchen keeping an eye on a three-bean chili, while he shows Eric how to make the regular white bread into garlic bread. Mom is on the couch, feet up, eyes closed.

"How are you doing, honey?" she says when I walk into the room. She always knows it's me, somehow.

"Fine." I grab plates from the cabinet and set them on the table. She opens her eyes and looks at me. "I got an email from that nonprofit."

"The one for your community service? That's good." She smiles. "I'm proud of you for taking care of that. I know it hasn't been easy getting all your requirements in order."

I shrug.

"Jen? You need anything?" David leans on the door.

"I'm okay, sweetie." They smile at each other.

Once dinner is on the table, we chow down. Mom asks me about the mentorship program, and I tell her a little more.

"Do you think they'll pair you with a trans kid?" David asks, gently tapping Eric's elbow so he takes it off the table.

"Maybe." I haven't given it much thought since I turned the form in.

"I bet they will," Mom says. "I bet there's some non-binary ten-year-old out there who would love a buddy like you."

"Yeah, then you wouldn't be bugging us all the time," Kevin says through a mouthful of bread.

"Right, because I love hanging out with twelve-year-old wannabe Marines." I roll my eyes.

"I think it'll be good for you," Mom says. "You can get involved, make a difference in the community."

"I guess." I chug some milk to cool the burn of the chili. Do I want to make a difference? I don't know. Some of my friends do. They show up for every protest in Seattle, participate in student groups, go to Pride events. But I've never been into that stuff. I had to be someone I wasn't for sixteen years. I just want to relax and be comfortable for a while.

On Sunday, David drops me off at the volunteer orientation for Northwest Pride. It's in a huge new building across the street from Cal Anderson Park, down a hallway and through a frosted glass door. Inside, the walls are painted golden yellow, and a smiling young man greets me from the reception desk. He directs me to a conference room, and when I push open the door, twelve people swivel their heads to look at me.

"Parker?" The presenter, a tall woman with a rich, warm voice, consults her clipboard.

"That's me." I find an empty seat at the far end of the table.

"Welcome! Now that we're all here, how about a round of names and pronouns?"

The training is an hour long. Mission statement, history, how the program works, what to expect, ideas for buddy hangouts: She covers it all. I take notes, feeling nervous for the first time. Some of the other volunteers have experience working with kids: they've been babysitters, or had summer jobs as camp counselors. I don't have anything. What am I supposed to say to a kid I've never met? What if my buddy doesn't like the activities I pick?

And another problem: the program isn't enough to cover my community service hours. We can see our buddies a maximum of twice a week, four hours each. The presenter explains this is the best balance they've found, so the program doesn't cross the line into unpaid childcare.

But that doesn't cover all the hours I need.

After the training, I approach the presenter.

"Hey," I say, reading her nametag. "Alicia. I'm doing this for community service hours." Uh-oh. That sounds bad.

But she's nodding. "Lots of people do."

"Cool." I smile. "So the thing is, even with the program, I still need to do thirty hours."

"Well, you know, we have a lot of other needs here." She grabs a volunteer pamphlet and hands it to me, along with a business card. She's the volunteer coordinator. "If you see something else you'd like to do, feel free to email me."

I nod and head out. The sun is shining outside, filtering through the leaves on the trees surrounding the park. I cross the street and sit on the low wall at the park entrance, looking around while I wait for David. During the orientation, Alicia said we'd get our buddy assignments Monday. I kind of hope I do get a trans kid. If I'd known any trans people when I was little, maybe it would have made a difference for me. Maybe I wouldn't have spent so long trying to get myself to like tight jeans and low-cut shirts. Maybe I would have understood why my skin crawled whenever anyone called me miss, or girl, or she.

I'm not a she. "She" is a basketball clanking off the rim without going in. "They" is the roar of the crowd when I make a shot. I might be playing on the girls' team, but when I'm on the court, I'm just Parker.

My name echoes from the street. David's there in our ancient station wagon. Once I'm in the car, he raises his eyebrows.

"So. We watching the game tonight?"

"I don't know. Am I gonna have to explain the rules again?" I smirk and he swats his hand in my direction. David never played sports, so he doesn't really understand why I love the Seattle Storm so much, why watching a game gets me so hyped up. But he wants to spend time with me, and he listens while I rant about player stats. It's nice. I don't see my dad much now that he lives in Florida, and he never showed much interest in me or what I like anyway.

So maybe David doesn't get basketball. But he tries. That's enough.

"I can't believe this!" Stella shrieks at her phone screen.

"What happened now?" I ask. Stella is always upset about something, and it's usually political.

"The principal keeps stalling on gender-neutral restrooms," she says, flipping back her curly red hair. The fresh sunburn on her nose stands out against the pale white skin of her cheeks. "We went to see him again last week, with a petition signed by, like, two hundred people." Stella is the president of the Queer Alliance. "He said he'd change the signs by Friday and make them available to students, but he didn't." She leans over and shows me a photo someone texted her: the single-stall staff bathrooms, still labeled "Men" and "Women." Under that, "Adults Only."

I shrug. "Maybe he just didn't get around to it."

"What? Come on, Parker. We've been talking to him for months now. I thought you of all people would care."

I frown. Stella means well, but she's always saying stuff like that. As if I'm a representative for all non-binary people. I don't like using the girls' restroom all the time, but I'm used to it. It's not the worst thing in the world. And most people think I'm a girl anyway. I don't really feel like I have the right to demand an all-gender bathroom. I'm not the kind of person who needs it most.

She catches my look and sighs. "I'm sorry. I didn't mean it that way."

"You did, though."

"Don't be mad. I'm sorry. I'm just frustrated." She glares at the phone. "Washington State prohibits discrimination on the basis of gender identity. And the school district mandated the availability of alternative restrooms to students. He's breaking the law!"

"So call the police." I'm trying to joke, but she turns her glare on me.

"Cops are not our friends," she says.

"I know that. I only suggested it because he's white," I say. "Nothing would happen to him." Soon after their engagement, Mom and David gave me the Talk about police brutality and racism. How my new brothers wouldn't ever have the same experience I did with cops, and how I needed to think twice anytime I thought police might be helpful to our family. I never forgot how it felt to watch David choke up as he talked to me.

"I just don't know what it's going to take," Stella says. "We need all-gender restrooms at this school."

"It'll happen." I nudge her elbow with mine. But she just shakes her head, biting her lip, and stares off down the hallway.

I get the email that night: "Youth4Youth Buddy Assignment," the subject line reads, with rainbow flag emojis on either side. I open it, a sudden burst of nerves making my heart pound.

My buddy is a nine-year-old named Xavier. He's a fan of comics, skateboarding, and lady pop stars. I smile at that last one. I love when kids say fuck it to gender stereotypes. Reading on, I learn more about his family: a single mom who works at Target, and an older sister in high school.

The next line turns my nerves into excitement: *You were matched with Xavier because he specifically requested a trans mentor.* So he must be trans too. Except, a trans boy, because of the pronouns. Or maybe not. I know a few nonbinary people who use binary pronouns.

Either way, I'm excited now. I imagine pushing him on the swings while he laughs. Him cheering for me from the sidelines at a basketball game. Him asking me for advice on coming out. Kevin and Eric are cool, as siblings go: they respect my pronouns, they make fun of me like they would anyone else, and they don't joke about identifying as an attack helicopter. Kevin even told off one of his friends once. But I know they don't get it. Not that they need to. Still, I wish I had someone as close to me as my family who really understood. Maybe I can be that person for Xavier.

Now that I have something new to look forward to, the week crawls by. Right after I got my buddy assignment, I emailed Xavier's mom. She got back within an hour, email full of exclamations and smiley faces, and we made a plan to meet up on Saturday. My first buddy hangout has to be observed by a Northwest Pride staff member, so I chose something I thought would make a good impression: the skate park. It's something Xavier likes, it's active, and something I don't know anything about. That means we'll have plenty to talk about. Maybe he can even teach me to skate.

Friday night, I knock on Kevin's doorway. His door is open and he's on his computer, engrossed in some online fantasy RPG. "Hello. Earth to Kev." He's dead to the world, eyes fixed to the screen, back to me. "Come in, Kev." I cross the room and grab him in a headlock, grinding my fist through his fuzzy Afro down to his skull.

"Get off me!" He flails and I let go, laughing.

"Can I borrow your board tomorrow?"

He swivels, eyebrows raised. "You're going skateboarding? Since when?" I tell him about Xavier and he nods. "So all the times I begged you to take me skating and you said no, and now you want my board?"

"Come on, Kev."

"Five dollars."

"Are you serious?"

He gives me a blank-faced stare. "You wanna roll like me, you gotta pay the fee." He starts beatboxing and I can't help grinning.

"Fine." I dig out the five-dollar bill I brought just in case.

He crows, grabbing it from me, then bounds to his closet, digs around for a minute, and hauls out his skateboard.

"Thanks, bro." I take it from him. He waves me off and turns back to his game.

Saturday dawns warm and sunny. The park is across from the library, with a deep bowl at one end, surrounded by a flat concrete plaza, curbs and rails of various heights scattered around. A group of older guys sits on the opposite side from me, a few of them zooming in and out of the bowl. A smaller boy grinds loudly down a rail, stumbling off at the end.

I look around. There's a couple moms with strollers, an old man smoking on a bench.

"Parker?" I turn and see a short, curvy woman, a big smile on her face.

"Hi." I lift a hand, but she's already spreading her arms, and suddenly we're hugging.

She steps back, still smiling. "I'm Leanne. Xavier's mom."

"Oh, yeah! Hi. How are you?" I scan behind her, but I don't see any kids.

"Just great. I'm so glad to meet you. We've been talking about you all week." She points at the bowl. "That's my kiddo."

The small boy I'd seen on the rail a minute before is now at the bowl's edge. He tips down and disappears, then sails up the other side and back down again. He's skinny, with olive-brown skin and floppy black hair smashed onto his forehead by a helmet.

She looks up at me as we watch him. "I'm just so excited for him. We were hoping that his mentor would be trans, but honestly I'm just happy for him to have anyone in his life from the gay community."

"Oh." I glance over at her. Maybe Northwest Pride didn't tell her. "I'm, uh. I am trans."

"Really?!" She looks at me again and does that eye-flick cis people do, where they check out my chest and then my face, like they're searching for something: evidence, maybe. "I had no idea."

"I'm nonbinary. I was assigned female at birth. My pronouns are they/them." I haven't had this conversation in a while, and the words are stiff and awkward.

"Oh, great! I've never met a nonbinary person before." She laughs lightly. "Well. He'll be excited."

Xavier rolls to a stop in front of us. "Are you Parker?"

"That's me." I extend a fist for him to bump, and he does, gazing up at me from behind his long bangs.

"They're nonbinary, sweetie," Leanne says.

"Cool." Xavier doesn't smile. "Do you skate?"

I heft Kevin's board in one hand. "I was hoping you could teach me."

"Well, you're wearing the wrong shoes." He points at my Nikes.

"You used to skate in sneakers," Leanne says.

He scans me up and down, taking in my bright white basketball shorts, my baggy Seattle Storm T-shirt with its rolled-up sleeves, my black snapback, and my hair, tied in a low pony.

"How come you have long hair?" he asks.

"I like it."

He nods. "Come on." Dropping his board, he zooms back toward the bowl. I look at Leanne and she nods.

"I'll just be over there," she says, pointing to a bench. I look and see Alicia, who waves at me.

When I join Xavier, he's balancing on the side edge of his board, the other edge on the sidewalk, trying to flip it.

"Okay. First we have to figure out whether you're goofy or not." He points at my feet.

I know that term. Even though Kevin acts like I never did anything for him, I definitely took him to the skate park a few times back in the day. I set my right foot on the board.

"You are. That's cool. Most people aren't." He still looks so serious. Does this kid ever smile?

"Okay, so push off like this." He knocks his board over onto its wheels, sets his left foot on it, and pushes off with the right.

Doesn't seem that hard. I imitate him, pushing a few times before swinging my back foot onto the board like I've seen Kevin do.

"I did it!" I spread my arms wide and he circles out and around, looking over at me.

"You have to bend your knees more."

I obey, and start curving toward the benches, losing speed.

"Turn!" he calls out.

How do I turn? The benches are feet away. I don't know how to stop.

Crack! My shins hit wood and I land on my ass on the concrete as the board slides under the bench. I sit there, massaging my legs.

Xavier rolls up. "You should have turned."

I close my eyes and open them. "Yep, I got that."

"Sorry."

"Nah. It's fine. Let's go again." I stand up slowly and hobble to my board.

We spend the afternoon skating. I manage to master turning on my board after only five more falls, earning a knee scrape that makes Xavier suck in his breath. Eventually, we take a break, sitting on the bench and watching a new group of skaters take over the bowl. There's even a few girls skating — people I assume are girls, anyway. I know from experience that looks don't always equal gender.

"So your mom mentioned you wanted a trans mentor," I say, because it's the first thing that comes to mind.

He nods. "Can I ask what bathroom you use?"

I look down at him. He's watching the skaters, skinny shoulders drowning in a bright red Fox Racing shirt. "I use the girls' room," I say.

He wrinkles his nose. "Why?"

"Well, I'm nonbinary. The men's room isn't comfortable either. And I was socialized as a girl, so I'm just used to it." He nods. I lean back against the bench, enjoying the hot sun on my skin. "How about you?"

"I don't."

"Don't use the girls'?"

"I don't use the bathroom at school. I wait until I get home." He fiddles with his board, running his fingernail across the glittery black surface.

"Wow. I'm sorry."

He shrugs. "I don't want to be alone in there. The guys at school are mean. They still call me my old name."

I frown. "That's dumb. I think your name is really cool."

"Thanks. Do you like X-Men?"

I blink, wondering where he's going with this for a minute, and then I connect the dots. He named himself after Professor X. The leader of the mutants. I grin. This kid has a keen sense of irony.

"Yeah," I say. "I've only seen the movies, though."

"What?!" He turns to me, mouth open, the biggest display of emotion I've seen all day. "That's ridiculous! I'll bring you some comics next time."

I laugh. "Sounds good."

"Xavier, honey. Time to go." Leanne leans on the back of the bench. Alicia is nowhere in sight. "She had to go," Leanne adds as I look around. "But she said to tell you 'great job.'"

We make a plan for Thursday, and they head out of the park, toward a battered Subaru. I drop my board, set my right foot down, and skate toward the bus stop.

School drags on toward the end of the year, but for once, I don't mind. Let time slow down. Maybe then I can complete community service on time. Between my hangouts with Xavier every week, and two hours every evening stuffing envelopes at the Northwest Pride office, I figure I can cover it. Barely.

By the third-to-last week of school, I'm struggling. Volunteering means I stay up late to finish homework. And then I'm in class, like today, resting my chin on my cupped hands so my fingers can hold up my eyelids without anyone noticing.

I excuse myself for the bathroom. Maybe a walk will wake me up.

The hallways are empty, sun pooling on the blue-and-white linoleum. The familiar hum of irritation whirs to life in my brain as I approach the bathroom doors. At the door to the girls', I stop. Usually I'd just push right through the doors, but today I'm angry. Why do I have to choose? Cis people seem to think a sign on a door will keep them safe, but I'm not safer in a gendered bathroom. I've seen the looks cis women give me when they think I'm a teenage boy. And good fucking luck to me trying to use a men's bathroom.

Deep breath. I walk in and head for a stall. I think of Xavier, holding his pee all day just to avoid making the choice: bury his real self five minutes at a time and risk ridicule or worse, or embrace his real self and risk ridicule or worse. Which is safer? Which is better? Which one might get you a world of hurt, and which one definitely will?

There's no way to know.

At lunch, I find Stella in the library with some of our other friends. They're working on posters. I read one over her shoulder: #PEEQUALITY FOR ALL, in bright orange marker.

"I hate that slogan," Tristan says, rolling his eyes. "It sounds like they're talking about the quality of my urine, not my bathroom rights."

I snicker.

"Come on, guys," Stella says. "This is serious."

Tristan catches my eye and grins. "You're such a good ally, Stel, we should make you an Honorary Trans."

She rolls her eyes. I pull up an empty chair next to Lexie, who smiles at me from behind a curtain of blond hair before returning to the elaborate drawing of an anime girl on her poster.

Stella shoves poster paper and markers at me. "I know you don't want to be part of a protest, but do you want to make signs?"

I shrug. "Why not?"

She raises her eyebrows. I pretend not to notice, selecting a dark blue marker from the pile. "So I'm guessing no gender-neutral restrooms yet."

"Nope. So the Queer Alliance is holding a sit-in in the principal's office next week." Stella smiles.

"What time?"

She tilts her head. "We're going in at lunch, when he's gone. Why?"

"Just curious."

"Wait. Are you going to come?"

I keep my eyes fixed on my poster and shrug again. She snorts, and I feel the irritation rise. She thinks she knows me, but she doesn't. She can hold protests all she wants, but she'll never understand what it feels like to be trans in a world that wants to erase you.

On Sunday, I go over to Xavier's house. It's small and beige, the yard surrounded by a chain-link fence. When I knock on the door, Leanne lets me in.

"Parker! The new issue is here!" Xavier appears from a room down the short hallway to the back of the house. He's got an X-Men comic in one hand. "You have to catch up."

"Wanna read outside?"

He nods.

The backyard is in full sun, except for a gnarled apple tree casting a circle of shade onto the yellowed grass.

We spread a blanket and he plops down, instantly lost in the comic. I pick the next one from the stack of issues he brought out for me and start reading.

I've never been much for comics, but the X-Men are fun. My favorite is Mystique, who can shape-shift into anything she wants. I wish I could do that.

We read for a long time, until the shadows move and the sun starts creeping onto our blanket. Xavier runs inside and comes out with chips and juice.

"How's school?" I ask.

"Almost over."

I choke on my juice from laughing, and he watches me, confused. "What's so funny?"

I shake my head. "Nothing. You're right. It is."

"Mom's transferring me to a new school next year," he says. "This one has trans kids like me."

"That's great." I high-five him. "And hopefully no ass-holes. I mean, jerks."

"You can say that word," he says, rolling his eyes. "I've heard it before."

"Are you excited?"

He shrugs. "I just hope I can use the bathroom there."

"My friends are trying to get gender-neutral rest-rooms at our school right now," I say. "What do you think of that?"

He pops a chip in his mouth, picking at the grass.

"That's cool. I don't want to use a gender-neutral restroom, though. I want to use the boys' bathroom."

"It's a good start, though. And then I won't have to pick."

"Oh, yeah!" He nods. "I forgot."

The breeze blows around us, warm and soft. I sip my juice. Should we do something else? Is he getting bored?

"Want to go play basketball at the park?" he asks.

I grin. "Only if you're ready to lose."

For the first time, a smile sneaks onto his face.

As the day of the sit-in approaches, I'm nervous. For the first time in my life, I want to join a protest, but I don't know what to expect. Logically, I know nothing bad will happen. We're just occupying the principal's office. At most, I'll get a detention, maybe a suspension. And I'm white. I won't face consequences as harsh as some other kids might.

But speaking up means giving up my anonymity. I won't be just Parker, that nonbinary kid who no one remembers is nonbinary. I'll be Parker, that nonbinary kid who was at the protest. Who wants gender-neutral restrooms. Who wants to change the way things are done at school. What happens once your name and face are out there? What happens when the people who don't want things to change know who you are?

At lunch, I head for the gathering spot: the T where the front hallway meets the hallway to the main office. A group of kids are already there, signs rolled up at their sides, talking in a low buzz. I slip in beside Tristan. He gives me a head nod and a fist bump.

We move toward the office at some invisible signal. Stella's in the front, leading us in, ignoring the secretary's raised voice, pushing through the swinging door into the back hallway toward the principal's office. I've never been back here before, and my heart is pounding, but I'm surrounded by people. Too late to back out now.

The office is empty and we crowd in, covering the floor, a few kids perching in the chairs. Stella stands behind the principal's desk.

"What's going on?" the secretary asks. "You can't be back here."

"This is a protest," Stella says. "Mr. Carter promised he would change the staff restrooms into gender-neutral restrooms, and he hasn't followed through. We aren't leaving until he does."

"Absolutely not." The secretary shakes her head. "You can come back and petition him in a small group."

"We already did that," Tristan says beside me.

The secretary sputters, glaring first at him, then at me. "I'm calling Mr. Carter."

"Good!" Stella says. "You do that."

She starts chanting, and the other kids follow suit. Tristan claps along, but doesn't chant. I just watch.

The principal appears a few minutes later, the top of his bald head almost brushing the ceiling outside the door. The chanting subsides.

"Well, it's not every day you can say you've been protested," he says with a chuckle. No one laughs.

"We're not leaving until you change the bathrooms like you promised," Stella says.

He smiles. "I know it's slow, but I'm working on it. Don't worry."

"How hard is it to change some signs?" another boy pipes up from the back wall.

"Here, we printed some up." Stella waves a stack of papers with the All-Gender Restroom logo on them. "The custodian said he could take down the other signs and put these up as soon as you say the word."

Mr. Carter's face darkens from white to ruddy, lips pressed together. "It's not that simple."

"It is that simple." Stella's on her soapbox. I want to tell Mr. Carter to give in now, while he still has his dignity. "By refusing to change the signs, you are landing on the wrong side of history. Seattle mandated all-gender restroom signage on public single-stall restrooms almost three years ago. And you're breaking our state's anti-discrimination law, which protects transgender students and their bathroom access. There are students at this school who every day feel the consequences of that decision. Kids who don't feel safe in gendered restrooms. Kids who have to choose between one or the other."

"She took the words right out of my mouth," Tristan mutters in my ear. It's a joke, but neither of us is laughing. I know Stella wants to help, but watching her stand there and talk when I'm right here, Tristan is right here, Lexie is right here, actually experiencing the things she's using for her moment of defiance? Anger rushes through my body in a wave of heat.

"Parker deals with that every day!"

Huh? I surface through the frustration and see her, hand extended to me, and then Mr. Carter, turning his stare in my direction. I open my mouth, but Stella keeps right on talking. I try to stay focused on what's happening, try to tell myself she means well, she's helping, but a tide of anger rises in my chest.

Mr. Carter holds up his hands. "All right, Ms. McMahon. I've heard enough." He smiles, but it's forced this time. The counselors and the office staff are gathered behind him now, and I spot Ms. Kerry over his shoulder. He looks back at them, then reaches for the phone on the wall, dialing a number.

The room is silent. He's probably calling security, and we're all going to be written up.

"John? Yes. Hello. Could you change those signs we

discussed?" He nods around at the room, and everyone's mouths are opening, people turning to look at each other. "Wonderful. No, that won't be necessary. I've got some printouts on hand."

He hangs up the phone and spreads his hands. "Now, may I have my office back?"

We spill out into the hall, everyone chattering at once, shrieking and hugging. Stella grabs my arm.

"You came!" she says. "I can't believe it worked! I can't believe I stood up to him like that!"

"Yep." I nod.

"What's wrong?" We face each other, the group carrying on down the hall without us. "Aren't you happy about this?"

I sigh. "Yes."

"So?" She's got that look on her face, the one I know means she won't let this go until I say something.

"You kind of . . . took over."

"I'm the president of the Queer Alliance." She stands, hands on hips, waiting.

"But you're not trans."

"No one else was speaking up."

"Because you didn't give them a chance."

She scoffs. "Right, because you've been so ready to put yourself out there."

"You used my name!" My voice comes out louder than

I intended, and she steps back. "You used me as an example. Like I'm just some stand-in for all the poor, oppressed trans kids at school. You pointed me out by name. Carter looked right at me. You never asked me if I wanted to be put on the spot. You just did it. Like you just do everything. Did you ever ask Tristan if he wanted to speak instead of you? Or Lexie?"

Her mouth is open, but she doesn't say anything. She just stares at me, eyes filling with tears, face bright red. The bell rings and she turns abruptly, marching away from me through the oncoming crowd. I hate that I feel guilty for yelling at her when I know everything I said was true. But I've never said anything to her before. Deep down, I felt like she wouldn't be able to hear it. And it looks like I was right.

Stella and I don't speak for the rest of the week. When Mom gets home Friday afternoon, I'm sprawled on the couch, staring at the ceiling.

"You look as tired as I feel," she says, dropping her purse on the table. Her scrubs today are bright purple. I shrug. She makes like she's going to sit on my outstretched legs and I swing them up out of her way, then set them on her lap.

"What are the headlines for the weekend?" she asks.

"Teen tells off friend who deserves it, gets put in friend jail for life," I say.

"Stella finally went too far, huh?"

I lay out the story and she shakes her head. "I admire her passion, but she needs to learn not everything is about her."

"So I didn't fuck up? Mess up. Sorry."

She waves her hand. "Maybe the raised voice was a bit much. But if it was me, I probably would have yelled too."

"I just don't know what to do now." I cross my arms. "I didn't do anything wrong, but how do I get her to talk to me again without apologizing?"

"You don't think she'll come around?" Mom watches me. I make a face. "Well. I would be surprised if ten years of friendship could go down the drain that fast. Whatever happens, I'm proud of you. Sounds like you took a stand in multiple ways this week."

I smile. I've used the gender-neutral restrooms every day since the protest, and every time I feel lighter. When I'm alone in those little rooms, washing my hands, looking in the mirror, I think about Xavier. How maybe he'll come to our high school one day and he won't have to worry. How even if people are shitty to him about the boys' bathroom, he'll still have an option. Thinking about it makes me feel like I'm part of history, like I made a difference in some way, pushed back against the bullshit. I understand why Stella is so passionate about social change. Even if she does need to learn when to step back.

*　　*　　*

"Parker! Parker!" I spot Xavier as soon as I get to the skate park that weekend. He zooms toward me, ollying over a curb.

"Nice!" I yell back. I drop Kevin's board and push off toward him.

"Are you ready to learn to jump today?" he asks as we circle. I pull a face. "Come on! You promised."

"I'm scared!" I exaggerate a grimace, mouth wide like a carved pumpkin.

He rolls his eyes, smiling. "You'll be fine."

"Okay, okay. Taskmaster." I follow him over to an empty section of the plaza.

"Maybe this summer, you can actually go in the bowl," he says.

This summer. I'll be graduated. Hopefully. Which means no more community service. I've been so caught up that I haven't even thought about what happens with Xavier and me once school is over.

"Maybe," I say, because the silence is stretching too long.

He tilts his head.

I'm balancing on my board, but it feels like I'm on the edge of a cliff. "I might not be volunteering this summer."

"What? Why?" His voice is shrill.

I explain about my community service hours. When I finish, his face is blank.

"Xavier?"

He zips away from me.

He's fast, but I have the hang of skating now, and I follow him around the park, until he sits on a bench, arms crossed. He doesn't look at me when I sit down next to him.

"Are you upset with me?" I ask. Even though I know he is. There's a horrible twisting feeling in my stomach. I wish I'd thought about this sooner, wish I'd figured out what I want after I graduate.

"Leave me alone." He turns away from me.

I look around. His mom sits on the other side of the park, talking on her phone. I don't know what to do.

"I might keep volunteering," I say. "I don't know yet."

"Why would you? You only needed to graduate."

The words sting, but he's right. I can't think of anything to say.

He stands up, not looking at me. "I want to go home."

"Okay."

I watch him trudge across the park to Leanne. She pauses in her conversation as he talks to her, then looks up at me, tilting her head in a question, the same way Xavier does. I turn up my hands and she shrugs, waving to me as they walk toward the car. Xavier doesn't look back.

The last week of school rolls in. I've been volunteering at Northwest Pride on weekends too. Those shifts, plus after school, plus my weekly four-hour hangouts with Xavier, will be enough. I hope.

Every time I think of Xavier, I feel like the world's worst person. I emailed his mom to explain what happened, and she understood, but it didn't feel like enough.

I'm still so tied up in guilt that I don't even notice the messenger come in to fourth period on Wednesday. The instant I hear my name, I know what's happening.

When I walk into Ms. Kerry's office, she doesn't look up, fixed on whatever she's typing. A few excruciating minutes later, she lifts her head. "Parker. Good to see you. Still protesting?"

I smile. "There's a lot of stuff left to change."

She smiles back. "Speaking of change." Her fingers tap the keys on her laptop and she spins it toward me. At first, I'm not sure what I'm looking for, but then I see it: the number under the community service hours category.

Sixty-two.

I did it.

I made it.

"I'm graduating?" I look up at her, and she nods.

"Good work," she says.

I let out a whoop and pump my fist, surprising a laugh out of her.

"I hope you enjoyed your community service," she says. "Alicia had wonderful things to say about you."

"I did," I say. "I really did." Xavier and I went to the water park for one of our hangouts, screaming our way down the slides. I'd never had that much fun swimming before. Usually I'm too in my head about all the ways I wish my body was different. But not that time.

My heart hurts when I think of Xavier. He's the reason I'm graduating. His face flashes in my mind, the way the playful light in his eyes vanished when he found out why I was volunteering. I want to see him, want to apologize.

When the bell rings, I head for the usual spot, making it all the way down the hall before I spot Stella sitting there and stop.

She still isn't talking to me. I start to turn, but she looks up and we lock eyes.

There's a long moment of what would be silence, if the halls weren't full of yelling kids, and then she stands up.

"Hey," she says.

I raise my hand in greeting.

"Are you still mad at me?" she asks, so quietly I have to step closer to hear her.

I think for a minute as she watches me. "Not exactly." Her face starts to fall. "I mean, what you did was pretty frustrating. I know how passionate you are, but I just wish you would let other people take the lead sometimes. It's not all about you."

Her face is turning red again, her eyes glassy. This is it. I've really done it this time.

But then she nods. "I know," she says, voice small and watery. "I'm sorry."

I nod. We stand there. I don't know what to do next, and she still looks like she's going to cry. So I change the subject.

"I'm graduating after all," I say.

Her eyebrows jump up to her hairline. "No way." She covers her mouth. "Oh shit, I'm sorry, I'm sorry!"

I laugh. "It's all good. I didn't think I was going to either."

She smiles, and we sit down and start talking.

Graduation passes in a whirl of gowns and flashing cameras, Mom and David waving from the stands. The weekend after, I wake up expecting to feel happy, but I don't.

I keep thinking about Xavier. He's not just a buddy to me. He's a third brother. My trans little brother. I think about us skating, him bossing me around, the questions he asks all casual, like they don't really mean anything, but I know they do. They're the questions I wish I'd been able to ask someone at his age.

I send off an email to Leanne, not knowing if it will matter, but knowing I have to try. If I'm going to help make the world a better place, I have to own my fuck-ups, not just ride the protest wave.

He's still pretty mopey, Leanne writes back. *But he didn't say no to a meet-up. The usual place and time?*

The next day is Sunday, and I take the familiar bus ride, board in hand. I'm nervous, stomach surging and rolling.

The park is busy, but I see them right away. Leanne ruffles Xavier's hair as I approach and kneel down so we're almost eye to eye.

"I'm still mad at you," he blurts out before I can say anything.

"That's okay. I'd be mad too if I were you," I say.

His small, dark eyebrows rise.

I take a deep breath. "Xavier. I'm not going to stop being your buddy."

He's silent, fiddling with his own board. If he brought it, that must be a good sign.

"Do you believe me?" I ask.

"Why would you if you don't have to?" He stares at the park, jaw clenched, and suddenly I feel like I'm going to cry.

"Because I like you, kid."

"I'm not a kid," he says, but he half turns his head toward me.

"I like being your buddy. Yeah, part of the reason I started volunteering was for my hours. But I did this program because I wanted to, and I love hanging out with you."

"Really?" He looks up at me, frowning.

I nod. "Yeah. I'm sorry. I should have been up front with you from the beginning."

"That would have been nice." He scuffs his shoe on the ground. "I mean, I know about high school stuff. My sister had to do volunteer hours too. But still."

"Still. I could have told you." I hold out a fist, and a long moment passes. And then he raises his fist and bumps mine. Relief floods my body. "I promise, in the future, I will be honest with you about everything."

"Okay." He looks back at the bowl, where skaters rise and fall in the sunlight. "So are you ready to jump now?"

I laugh. "You're relentless!"

He smirks at me. "Mom says I'm determined." Leanne chuckles.

I stand up, board in hand. "Okay, Xavier. Show me how it's done."

UNTITLED

BY JASON REYNOLDS

there is nothing
on the road between memphis
and jackson
there is nothing
but big sky
and fields of green bristle
and flags hanging
hanging
star crossed
star-crossed
and there is nothing
that can stop me
from thinking
about whether or not
my DNA is in the dirt
out there
if there are tributaries
of my juvenile blood

running like veins
bubbling beneath earth's scalp
if the spirits of my folks
have caught the wind
out there
have caught wind
of my arrival
and limped the flags
just for me
just this once
to keep me brave
there is nothing
that can stop me
im thinking
there is nothing
that can stop me
im laughing
there is nothing
there is nothing
but the green grass
growing all around
all around

HOMECOMING

BY DARCIE LITTLE BADGER

IT TOOK THE ENTIRE SUMMER for Mama, Mom, and me to leave Paiute land. Moving is always like a puzzle in a puzzle. First, we packed our stuff, trying to fill every space in every box because there was no room to spare. Then we crammed our boxes into the back of our minivan, and when they didn't all fit the first time, we removed them and tried again. The whole process felt kinda like a ritual, as if my family was trading our time and sweat for a blessing.

The drive to Texas took way longer than it should have, since we stopped at every silly roadside attraction that advertised itself with a billboard along the highway. Mom considered herself an Instagram celebrity — her words, not mine — and never missed a chance to share pictures of oddities and good food with the four-hundred people following her account. Most of her followers were past friends and acquaintances; with every move, the count expanded. It always seemed strange to me that she wanted to stay in contact with them. As for me? The moment I left a place, I treated its people like memories. Things of the past that gradually fade away until they might as well be faceless, nameless extras in the movie of my life.

I was asleep when we finally reached home. That last day, we'd been on the road since dawn, and the sugar-and-caffeine rush from my lunchtime soda wore off by mid-afternoon. One moment, we were driving between a pair of soy fields, and my eyes felt heavy and the scenery was so monotonous that I figured I'd prop a pillow against the warm glass window and take a thirty-minute nap. The next thing I knew, Mama was saying my name and waking me up with a gentle shake.

"We're here," she said.

It was dark, but I could hear a thousand insects sing, feel warmth envelop me, and smell faint traces of campfire smoke and mesquite trees in the sluggish air. I stepped outside; the front headlights were still on, and they lit up our house like a pair of spotlights. The building was made from adobe brick, yellowish-orange blocks from the earth.

"What do you think?" Mama asked.

I didn't know what the rest of the town was like or whether our neighbors were nice. But I did know one thing: now that we were on Lipan land, I never wanted to leave.

"It's the best," I said.

It took us a week to completely unpack. One of the first things I did was look at paint swatches from the hardware store. I taped them on the bare white wall, these little squares of color.

I unpacked my clothes last; they were folded in two large boxes, and as I dug through my sweaters, shirts, dresses, and pants, I picked out a few candidates for my first-day-of-school outfit. I'd been thinking about that outfit all summer, wanting my first impression on Lipan to be a good one. Ultimately, I chose my favorite pair of jeans and a T-shirt screen-printed with the face of my third-favorite superhero, Silver Synapse. Both the pants and the shirt were loose enough to be comfortable and whole enough to comply with dress-code regulations (no holes, no bare shoulders, nothing above the knee, and no profanity). Plus, the T-shirt seemed like a good way to start conversations with other comic book readers. Part of me hoped that I'd meet a fellow Silver

Synapse fan, and by part of me, I mean the *really* optimistic part. He starred in a niche webcomic created by two art students, which meant that Silver Synapse wasn't Marvel-hero-level popular.

I couldn't have anticipated the fallout of my clever wardrobe choice.

My mom drove me to Pleasant Springs High School on the first day of school; she was still looking for work in town. I appreciated the gesture. I'd never had a pleasant bus ride, and some were downright upsetting. As Mom turned onto the street outside the school, we joined a drop-off line that was so long, it snaked around the parking lot. As we inched forward, she lowered the radio to a whisper. Always a sure sign of a Significant Talk.

"Check your bag," Mom said. "Did you leave anything behind?"

I laughed. "You mean since the last time I checked it? Before we left the driveway?"

"Just being cautious! You have my number. If you need . . ." She trailed off, distracted by a group of ten adults standing across the street from the high school property. They were lined up on the sidewalk, holding signs, the kind used at rallies or protests. I'd noticed the crowd earlier, but I'd assumed that they were over-enthusiastic parents waving "GOOD LUCK!!!" or "Yay learning!" banners. However, as our car crept closer to the group, a man turned his sign toward us. It was decorated with a brown-skinned head, in profile, with a smear of blue paint under its eye and eagle feathers in its braided hair. Beneath the head, the slogan "BRING BACK OUR BRAVE" was emblazoned across the poster board in red paint.

"Jesus H. Christ," Mom said. "What is all this?"

"I have no idea."

She started to lower the window. With a worried yelp, I patted her arm. "What are you doing?"

"I'm going to scold them."

"Mom, no! We're in a drop-off line. I don't want to be late."

"I can scold them and drive at the same time, like a multitasker."

"Can you just ignore . . . whatever that is? I don't want to be involved in an argument before first period begins."

She pursed her lips, as if locking up a slew of PG-13 curses, and obediently raised the window. "I wish you hadn't seen that nonsense," Mom said.

"It wouldn't be the first time."

As a rolling stone, I'd attended schools so large and bustling they were like ant colonies and schools so small that all the students knew each other by name. Pleasant Springs was small but not cozy; there must have been a thousand students in seventh through twelfth grade.

Despite the long drop-off line, I was ten minutes early. Rather than wander the halls or try to strike up a conversation with complete strangers in the hallway, I went straight to first period, introductory Spanish. Half the desks in the classroom were already occupied. After a moment's hesitation, I sat next to a blond girl in the middle row because I liked her red-framed glasses. She smiled and bent her fingers in a little wave.

"I'm Grace," I said, returning her smile. "What's your name? I mean. ¿Cómo te llamas?"

"Me llamo Naomi." Naomi gave me a quick once-over, and her smile immediately retracted into a concerned frown. "Are you with the protestors?" she asked, squinting at my T-shirt.

"Um. Wha . . ." I looked down, confused. Did somebody tape a sign on my chest? No. Silver Synapse smiled up at me. Sure, he was a Native character, but he looked nothing like the cartoon man on the protest signs. Like many superheroes, Silver Synapse wore a metallic gray mask over his eyes, and although his hair was braided, it had no feathers. How could Naomi mistake my T-shirt for "BRING BACK THE BRAVES" solidarity? "No!" I said. "Just. No. He's a superhero. An *Apache* hero. Created by Native artists. I bought this shirt at Indigenous Comic Con. Really, I have no idea what's happening across the street. What are they even protesting?"

"Wait. Are *you* Native American?" she asked, and now the once-over became a twice-over, this time lingering on my face.

"Lipan Apache of the Tcha shka-ózhäyê."

"How much are you?" she asked.

"Blood quantum isn't our thing," I said. "My mother is Lipan, so I am too." I didn't mention that I had two mothers; Naomi seemed nice, but not all people were open about their prejudices. I'd lived long enough to be wary.

"Those protesters are assholes," Naomi said.

"But what are they protesting?"

"The school mascot used to be an Indian brave," she said. "It was changed five years ago, because *obviously*, but that upset a bunch of old graduates. Every time there's an event, like a home game, *somebody* stands across the street with a sign. It makes you wonder how they have so much free time."

"Are you talking about the mascot people?" a brunette stranger asked. "They're embarrassing." She slid into the desk behind Naomi and leaned forward to talk, her two braids swinging over the desktop like a couple of pendulums.

"Yes," Naomi said. "This is Grace. She's actually Native American."

"I'm Hillary —" the girl started.

"Hey! Can you shut the fuck up?" asked a guy in plaid, interrupting Hillary's introduction; he sat at the front of the class a couple desks away. "My dad was part of this school before you were *born*. He's fighting for pride in traditions."

"Your dad was out there?" Hillary asked. "Crying about a racist mascot?" Naomi just turned bright red; she seemed to be on the verge of tears.

"Are you serious?" the guy asked. "My great-grandmother was Cherokee. The brave isn't racist. It's an honor."

"Uh. Jeremy. Didn't you say your great-grandparents came here through Ellis Island?" Hillary asked. "I *swear* I remember that from our family tree project last year."

"Keep my family tree out of your mouth."

As the class slipped into a heated argument, I slouched in my seat, hiding my shirt and waiting for the first-period bell to ring. In the hallway, strangers gave me dirty looks. Even worse, one boy whooped and shoved his hand in front of my face, expecting a high five. I sidestepped him, ducked into the nearest bathroom, and turned my shirt inside out, concealing the tags under my hair; that put an end to the negative attention.

Morning passed quickly; most of the lessons were easy, introductory fare, and a combination of day-one adrenaline and a restful summer kept me alert until lunch. My usual tactic for first-day lunches involved locating a familiar face and inserting myself into their group, but as I surveyed the cafeteria, I noticed a solitary girl sitting near the back wall. She was shoveling casserole into her mouth with one hand and holding open a book with the other. Her bearing was magnetic, 'cause I could empathize with a girl who ate and read at the same time. As I approached, I saw that the cover of her book was emblazoned with a serious-looking woman radiating green fire. "MAGIC IN CUBICLE NINE," the title read. "A CORPORATE PARANORMAL MYSTERY!" The girl, who wore a black hoodie and slate-gray jeans, glanced up when I sat across from her.

"Can I sit here?" I asked. *Please don't say no. Please don't say no. Please . . .*

She lifted a hand to cover her mouth and, her voice muffled by a half-chewed bite of noodles, said, "No worries. Go ahead."

I unclasped my tin lunch box and removed a sandwich, a bag of barbecue-flavored chips, and damp baby carrots. My lunch buddy lowered her book and watched me take a bite of turkey and cheese on rye.

"I never know how it's supposed to go," she said. "Sorry. Just thought you should be aware."

"How what's supposed to go?"

"Talking," she said. "What do people *usually* talk about? Sorry again. I can never think of anything."

"Don't apologize," I said. "Thanks for letting me sit here."

"Why wouldn't I?"

I shrugged. "It happens. Oh! Guess what. I brought something to read too." I rummaged through my backpack, which was already becoming disordered with loose leaves of paper and stray mechanical pencils. Despite all my good intentions to stay organized with color-coded notebooks and binders for each class, I knew that the system would fail within the first week. It always did. I found my paperback novel at the bottom of my bag, crushed beneath a geometry textbook that had been previously used by a student who'd highlighted half the text, as if the book was theirs; at least I had an indication of the important stuff.

When I sat up, my lunch buddy was buried in her urban fantasy again. She must have been at an exciting part. I didn't want to interrupt with more small talk; instead, I cracked open *Post-Postapocalypse*, a thriller set in the rebound of the end of the world. About five minutes later, my lunch buddy asked, "Is it good? *Post-a-postapocalypse*?"

"So far, yes. Fair warning: There's a lot of references to death. A man just fell into a swimming pool full of zombie heads. They ate him. Sort of. You can't eat without a body. Er. They chewed him to death."

"I don't mind horror," she said. "It's okay." After a pause long enough that I thought she'd returned to her own book, she added, "My name is Quinn."

From that point, the day only improved. In fact, when I stepped outside after the dismissal bell, the sky was blue, the air was warm, and the protestors had vanished. Apparently, they did have a life. Before long, my mama pulled up in her old van.

"Why is your shirt inside out?" she asked.

I threw my bag in the back seat and sat up front. "People kept getting the wrong idea. That's all."

Mama is no good at separating her emotions from her facial expressions, so her confusion expressed itself in a nearly comical eyebrow maneuver. To her credit, she didn't press me for more information. I figured I'd explain over supper, when I was less annoyed by the situation, by how I couldn't wear anything remotely Native without half the school mistaking it for mascot gear.

"When we get home," she said, "I want to show you where the garden will grow."

"You've already started?" I asked. She'd always wanted a garden. Not the frilly kind stocked with ornamental flowers and mass-produced vegetables from store-bought paper seed packets. A Lipan garden, an ecosystem of the edible and medicinal plants that had thrived on the land since the first people arrived.

"Just the planning stages. I want to get started before you're too busy with homework."

"I'll always have time to weed for you, Mama."

She laughed. "Leave the weeding to me. It's good exercise. You're a young woman now. You should learn how to grow food the right way. In a way that doesn't cause harm."

"Thank you," I said.

"Xásteyo," she corrected me. Although the federally championed genocide of my people had a terrible impact on our language, that expression of gratitude survived our darkest hour.

And I, born in the twenty-first century, agreed, "Xásteyo."

Group mentality is a strange thing. The Pleasant Springs mascot had been a ram for five years without much fuss — that's what Quinn informed me, anyway. But the year I came to town, the situation blew up. I couldn't help but feel like a spark in a tinderbox. Now, it may seem arrogant for a new kid with zero clout to take credit for any kind of climate-changing spark, but I observed a compelling pattern; arguments spawned around me. Arguments about the Indian brave, like the one between Hillary and Jeremy on my first day.

It was during one such argument that I learned about the first in-school protest. I was sorting the clutter in my locker when a high-pitched voice across the hall exclaimed, "You'll get suspended!"

"They'll have to suspend us all," a deeper voice said.

"So? You think Mrs. Reiland won't try?"

"Let her. My parents are lawyers."

"Taylor got penalized for exposing too much *shoulder*."

"That was against the dress code. This is a matter of free speech."

Somehow, I knew exactly what the pair were talking about.

It happened at the first Friday pep rally in the gymnasium, a cavernous room with bleachers along each of its long walls. Students were separated by grade; ninth and twelfth graders sat against one wall. Eleventh and tenth graders sat against the other. The seventh and eighth graders weren't invited. From my vantage point, I noticed a dozen cartoon braves glaring from the shirts and jackets of fifteen seniors. When the school mascot cartwheeled across the gymnasium, the Indian brave–wearing seniors stood in unison, their expressions a mixture of pride, amusement, and defiance.

For a moment, the room was mostly silent. Beside me, Quinn giggled in the way that people giggle at jump scares in horror movies.

Then, the tinder went ka-boom. A roar of seven-hundred voices, a cacophony of cheers and angry shouts, reverberated in the great domed chamber. The ram mascot shook his finger in the direction of the upperclassmen, as if scolding naughty children. Below me and to the right, Naomi of the red glasses gave the protesters the finger, bless her.

Rising above the noise, our principal's magnified voice said, "You lot. Sit down."

One of the seniors saluted her, but none sat down.

"Count of three," Principal Reiland said. "One. Two . . ."

"Or what?" one of them shouted at her, but he had no microphone, so she probably didn't hear the taunt.

"Three. Okay. All fifteen of you. Disciplinary room, *now*." The seniors took the long way down the bleachers, weaving through students instead of using the closest stairs. They flaunted the biggest grins, and a couple clasped their hands and shook them above their heads, like Olympic medalists celebrating a win.

Although they passed right in front of me, none of the protestors turned my way. If they had, I doubt they would have seen me.

"I hate people like that!" Quinn said. She practically shouted into my ear, but I could barely hear her voice.

"Yeah," I agreed.

"What?"

"I said, yeah! Me too!"

"Some people have real problems!"

"What was that?" I asked.

"Real problems! The world is going to shit. Literally what is the point? It's just a mascot."

"Just a what?"

"Just a mascot! Who cares?"

"You're talking about the seniors, right?"

The fifteen seniors who were waving goodbye and winking as they crossed the gymnasium, followed by a pissed-looking principal in a red-and-black pantsuit, the school colors.

"Everyone," Quinn said.

The roar had settled into a simmer of friendly conversation. Still, I had to ask, "What . . . did you say?"

"I said this is a bad look for *everyone*. It's a petty-ass town with no real fucking problems." She extracted a book from her jacket; technically, we weren't supposed to bring anything but ourselves to pep rallies, but Quinn was always prepared to read, even if it meant sewing an extra pocket into her liner.

I was glad she brought reading material. I didn't feel like talking to her anymore.

The best part about pep rallies was their end, because that's when everyone got to go home. That day, both my mothers were in the car. I had to take the back seat, which made me feel like a fancy person with two chauffeurs.

"We need to stop at the hardware store," Mama said. "The paint is ready."

"We also need caulk," Mom reminded her.

"And a slushie," I said. "From a drive-thru so I don't have to get out of the car and deal with people."

"I can get it for you," Mom volunteered. "People don't bother me."

"Thanks." As we pulled out of the high school parking lot, I noticed a crowd of parents and students congregating around the brick-and-bronze "PLEASANT SPRINGS: WELCOME" sign. Something was going down. "I wish there were drive-thru schools."

The next Monday morning, the sidewalk picketers were back, and their numbers had grown. I recognized some of the seniors who'd made a scene at the pep rally and the ten "Bring Back the Braves" forty-to-fifty-something-year-olds from the first day of school. But there were also other students, people I'd passed in the hallway, people who took classes with me. And there were more adults — parents, perhaps? Some sat in lawn chairs, as if settled in for the long haul.

I did my best to ignore them on the way into school and sat beside Naomi in Spanish class. "¿Cómo estás?" she asked.

"Así así."

"¡Lo siento, amiga!"

"Gracias."

"So, I'm in debate. . . ."

"¡En español, por favor!"

"Um. Yo . . . voy . . ."

"I'm only joking," I assured her. "What's up?"

She laughed. "You sounded *just* like Señor Favian. It was instinct. Anyway. Debate. Right. So you know the counterprotest after school on Tuesday?"

I shook my head. "No."

"Huh! Nobody mentioned it? Seriously?"

"I'm not well-connected. One drawback to being new."

"Yeah, but considering the subject . . ." She shrugged, as if dismayed. "Well, a bunch of us are showing support for the ram tomorrow. It's a whole thing. I think the city news will show up."

"Good," I said. "I was starting to feel outnumbered."

"Oh my god. No. Most people are on your side." She bit her lower lip. "I was wondering. Can you say something?"

"Huh?"

"I mean . . . can you speak at the rally tomorrow? Just for ten minutes. This whole incident affects you the most."

"You want my input."

"Yes!"

"Naomi." I spread my arms. "Can I hug you?"

She beamed. "Sure!"

I leaned over and gave her a one-armed squeeze, all the while wondering how I could possibly do my people justice with ten minutes of words. How could I succinctly voice our past, our present, and our future? Communicate every fiber of my being to strangers? How could I make them understand?

That's what I asked my mama that evening as we sat side by side on a new couch from the thrift store. Mom was dozing on her recliner, her mouth parted slightly in sleep. A late-night talk-show host babbled on the television, his voice an amusing form of white noise.

Mama had been beading my new eagle feather hair drop for the Nde Daa Pow Wow — according to the council, I was a strong candidate for STIDA Pow Wow princess next year, so she wanted my regalia to be perfect. At my question, she put her work aside, careful not to jostle the feather. Mama always handled our sacred feathers like they were newborns, as if she was afraid they'd fall apart and leave us with nothing again. There was a time when we, as state-recognized Natives, couldn't use the feathers in our ceremonies; it was against federal law. And by "a time," I mean as recently as 2014.

"I have no time to prepare either," I said, holding up my geometry textbook. "Two exercises due tomorrow. Plus, I need to read a chapter of world history and finish outlining my essay for English. Basically, I'm going to embarrass myself in front of everyone. Really wish Naomi could have clued me in before the weekend."

"If the speech is stressing you out," she said, "don't do it. Focus on homework. You're more important than a rally."

"Am I, though?" I asked.

Mama took my hand, and I was comforted by the warmth of my mother's palm, darker and more calloused than mine. Over my fourteen years alive, my hands had sprouted like a five-branched tree, elongating and shedding baby fat. But her hands? They'd been a constant in my life. How often did I watch them sew patches over the holes in my jeans? Pick me up when I fell down? Rock my cradle? Give me gifts and food? When Mama told me stories, her hands flitted through the air like they were part of her voice. I knew them better than I knew my own.

Now her hand squeezed mine firmly, as if saying, "I am here. I am always here to support you."

"Never question your importance," she said. "*Never.* You want resistance? Be proud of our people and *love yourself.* That is the most powerful way to fight the evil of colonialism."

"I'm always proud to be Lipan, Mama."

"Then why did you turn your shirt inside out on the first day of school?" she asked.

I pulled away from her. "That had nothing to do with pride. It was exhaustion! There was a superhero on my shirt, and people kept mistaking him for a mascot. And

I get it, okay? They thought he was a racist mascot 'cause mascots are how the dominant narrative wants to portray us. Obviously, that's messed up, which is why I'm doing this rally. But sometimes, I can't deal with everyone else's ignorance and bullshit 'cause I have my own life to worry about. Like on the first day of school, when I'm trying to learn a million new faces and lessons and how to walk from one end of the building to the other in five minutes with twenty pounds of books on my back and really don't want to start screaming in the middle of a busy hallway because complete strangers keep giving me nasty looks. I *do* love myself, Mama, which is why I turned my shirt inside out. Aren't I allowed to rest sometimes?"

Silence stretched between us, like punctuation at the end of my question.

"I'm sorry," she finally said. "I'm so sorry. Of course you are, Grace."

She pulled me into a hug.

"And I'm sorry I used the word bullshit, Mama," I said.

"Oh, don't apologize for that." She laughed. "You're just being truthful."

One day later, at 3:15 p.m., I stood on Lipan Apache land. My land. That day, I wore my mother's seed bead necklaces and the eagle feather hair drop she'd finished that night in lieu of sleep. The brown feather was accented with soft, fluffy down near its base and fastened to a leather-backed beaded circle that depicted a sun against a clear blue sky.

The ram rally, mostly students and teachers, filled the public park one block away from Pleasant Springs High. The Bring-Back-the-Braves-Something-Something-Free-Speech crowd also made an appearance, because of course they did. I ignored them during my beeline to the gazebo in the center of the park, where Naomi of the red glasses stood with a microphone in one hand and a sign declaring "RESPECT!" in the other.

"I'm ready, Naomi," I said. "Give me that microphone before my palms get too sweaty."

"I can't wait to hear you speak!" she said. "We just have to wait a liiiiittle longer."

"What for?" My mothers had promised me ice cream after the event, so I was eager to say my piece and flounce.

"Jeremy is your opposition. He said he'd be here —"

"Hold on," I said. "Opposition? You mean like a debate?"

Naomi blinked, her brown eyes wide behind the lenses she wore. "Yes. Didn't I mention that?"

"No! You're the one on the debate team. Not me!"

"It's not a *debate* debate," she said, her voice soft and ickly-sickly sweet. The kind of voice that should only be used to placate a fussy toddler. "Just. We're giving both sides a chance to be heard, you know? If you aren't comfortable, that's totally okay! I can take your place."

"And I can take that microphone." I plucked it from Naomi's hand and flipped the microphone switch from "off" to "on." The crackle that sputtered from the speakers silenced the crowd and drew their attention to the gazebo.

"Hóóyíí, Shizhách'i̓'íí ashíí Shitsi̱łki̓'i̱i̱!" I boomed. "My name is Grace. Like my mama, grandmothers, great-grandmothers, and great-great-grandmothers, I am Lipan Apache. To my Native siblings, mínì' níáá dààgǫ́ǫ́t̓í!"

I paused to look every Bring-Back-the-Braves protester in the eye.

"My humanity," I continued, "is not up for debate. Xásteyo."

With that, I descended the gazebo steps, taking the cordless microphone with me. The voices of the crowd were nothing but white noise. I'd said my piece. My mothers were waiting near the edge of the crowd, their expressions a mixture of concern and pride; both were extremely familiar to me.

"Well said," Mom said. She wore a wreath of flowers in her hair, white clover blooms tied together by their long green stems.

"Perfect!" Mama agreed. As she leaned in for a hug, I noticed that she wore a flower necklace; the petals tickled my chin. The two must have woven the jewelry in the park while I was busy with Naomi.

I plucked a flower from the clover patch beside my feet and, after a moment of consideration, tucked it behind my ear. You'll find clovers all over the place, from the East Coast to the West Coast (and beyond the sea), but the southern ones are unique. They're tough and unusually magnificent. Gotta be both to thrive on Lipan land. "Well," I said. "Ready to go home now?"

After ice cream, that's exactly what we did.

ACKNOWLEDGMENTS

THIS PROJECT WOULD NOT EXIST, if not for Beth Phelan, the intrepid and ambitious and always expansive rock star agent who found time between her own clients and industry-changing #DVpit to approach me about an activism-themed anthology. She and Louise Fury did the work of finding it a home, and I am forever grateful.

Thank you, Weslie Turner, for acquiring and helping shape this collection, and to Kait Feldmann, who came on board to help see it through. No one will ever outdo the jelly beans, I'm just saying. A huge thanks to Arthur A. Levine, and everyone on the team, for wanting this project, and believing in it.

A huge thanks to Jenn Baker, whose work is so heartfelt and impacting, and whose wisdom and advice was so generously given as I took on my first anthologist gig. Thank you for your generosity and support!

Obviously, I want to thank the contributors who poured out of themselves so that young people can see themselves. There is nothing in this collection that I don't adore, and by which I'm not totally impressed, and pleased to have had the opportunity to read before anyone else!

Thank you, Richie Pope, for your jaw-droppingly powerful cover!

I don't know quite how to say this last part, but I feel like it needs to be said: Thank you to the young people who've had to endure what they shouldn't have to, and for carrying on. You are doing the work of resistance, no matter how hard, and we draw strength to put down words in the hope that we can lighten your load, even a little.

CONTRIBUTOR BIOGRAPHIES

"ARE YOU THE GOOD KIND OF MUSLIM?"

SAMIRA AHMED (suh-MEE-rah ah-med) is the New York Times *bestselling author of* Love, Hate & Other Filters *(Soho Teen);* Internment *(Little, Brown Books for Young Readers); and* Mad, Bad & Dangerous to Know *(Soho Teen). She was born in Bombay, India, and grew up in Batavia, Illinois, in a house that smelled like fried onions, spices, and potpourri. A graduate of the University of Chicago, Samira has taught high school English in both the suburbs of Chicago and New York City, worked in education nonprofits, and spent time on the road for political campaigns. Her creative nonfiction and poetry have appeared in* Jaggery Lit, Entropy, *the* Fem, *and* Claudius Speaks *as well as the anthologies* This Is What a Librarian Looks Like, Who Will Speak for America?, *and* Color Outside the Lines. *Follow her online at samiraahmed.com and @sam_aye_ahm.*

KEAH BROWN *(key-uhh BROWN) is a journalist, freelance writer, and the creator of #DisabledAndCute. She is an advocate for people with disabilities and is from Lockport, NY. Her work has appeared on* Essence.com *and in* Teen Vogue, Catapult, Glamour, Harper's Bazaar, *and* Lenny Letter *among other publications.* The Pretty One *is her debut essay collection (Atria Books). Find her online at keahbrown.com and @Keah_Maria.*

L. D. LEWIS *(el dee LOO-iss) is author of speculative stories "Chesirah" and* A Ruin of Shadows. *She serves as a founding creator and art director of* FIYAH Magazine of Black Speculative Fiction. *In 2018, she was awarded the Working Class Writers Grant by the Speculative Literature Foundation. She lives in Georgia with her coffee habit, her cat, Gustavo, and an impressive FunkoPop! collection. Find her online at ldlewiswrites.com and @ellethevillain.*

"GRACE"
AND
"HOMECOMING"

DR. DARCIE LITTLE BADGER *(DAR-see lih-tul bah-jur) is a Lipan Apache geoscientist and writer who only plays chess with ghosts. Her short fiction has appeared in multiple places, including* Love Beyond Body, Space, and Time; Robot Dinosaur Stories; Strange Horizons; The Dark; Lightspeed; *and* Cicada. *Darcie's debut comic, "Worst Bargain in Town," was published in* Moonshot: The Indigenous Comics Collection, Volume 2. *She lives with one dog named Rosie and all of Rosie's toys. Find her online at darcielittlebadger.wordpress.com and @ShiningComic.*

"AURORA RISING"

YAMILE SAIED MÉNDEZ *(sha-MEE-lay sa-ee-EDH MEN-dez) is a fútbol-obsessed Argentine-American who loves meteor showers, summer, astrology, and pizza. She lives in Utah with her Puerto Rican husband and their five kids, two adorable dogs, and one majestic cat. An inaugural Walter Dean Myers Grant recipient, she's also a graduate of Voices of Our Nations (VONA) and the Vermont College of Fine Arts MFA Writing for Children and Young Adults program. She's the author of the picture book* Where Are You From? *(HarperCollins)* and the middle grade novels Blizzard Besties (Scholastic Press) and On These Magic Shores (Tu Books). She's also the children's lit guest editor at Hunger Mountain literary journal and a Pitch Wars middle grade mentor. Find her online at yamilesmendez.com and @YamileSMendez.

EDITOR
AND
"AS YOU WERE"

BETHANY C. MORROW (BETH-uh-nee cee mah-row) is the author of speculative stories that run the gamut between science fiction and speculative literary fiction. She is the author of Mem (Unnamed Press), an ABA Indies Introduce and Indie Next pick, and A Song Below Water (Tor). She is also a sensitivity reader. You can visit her online at bethanycmorrow.com and @BCMorrow.

"THE REAL ONES"

SOFIA QUINTERO (so-FEE-ah KEENG-tero) has published six novels and twice as many short stories, including the critically acclaimed "Efrain's Secret" and "Show and Prove." She earned an MFA in Writing and Producing Television from the TV Writers Studio at Long Island Univesity. As a 2017 Made in NY Writers Room Fellow, Sofia developed a TV show based on her 2006 novel Burn. *Her third YA novel is inspired by the call to #SayHerName. Find her online at sofiaquintero.com and sofiaquintero.*

JASON REYNOLDS *(JAY-sun reh-nolds) is a* New York Times *bestselling author, a Newbery Award Honoree, a Printz Award Honoree, a National Book Award Honoree, a Kirkus Award winner, a two-time Walter Dean Myers Award winner, an NAACP Image Award Winner, and the recipient of multiple Coretta Scott King honors. Reynolds was named the American Booksellers Association's 2017 and 2018 spokesperson for Indies First, and served as the national spokesperson for the 2018 celebration of School Library Month in April 2018, sponsored by the American Association of School Librarians (AASL). Jason's many works of fiction include* When I Was the Greatest, Boy in the Black Suit, All American Boys *(cowritten with Brendan Kiely),* As Brave As You, For Every One, Miles Morales: Spider Man, *the Track series (*Ghost, Patina, Sunny, *and* Lu*), and* Long Way Down, *which received both a Newbery Honor and a Printz Honor. He is on faculty at Lesley*

University, for the Writing for Young People MFA Program, and lives in Washington, DC. You can find his ramblings online at JasonWritesBooks.com.

LAURA SILVERMAN (lore-ah sil-ver-man) earned her MFA in Writing for Children at the New School. She is the author of Girl Out of Water and You Asked for Perfect. You can reach out on Twitter at @LJSilverman1 or through her website LauraSilvermanWrites.com.

"RUTH"

RAY STOEVE (RAY STO-vee) is a queer, non-binary writer from Seattle, Washington. They received a 2016–2017 Made at Hugo House Fellowship for their young adult fiction, and are on a personal mission to include at least one trans character in every book they write. When they're not writing heartfelt queer stories, they can be found working with youth, hiking their beloved Pacific Northwest, or on stage in drag. Find them online at raystoeve .wordpress.com and on Twitter at @raystoeve.

"PARKER OUTSIDE THE BOX"

CONNIE SUN *(KAW-nee SUN) is a cartoonist and writer, based in New York City. For seven years, she drew a daily webcomic strip every morning before going to her job at a university, where she ran education programs in conflict resolution. She has cartooned for the* New Yorker, McSweeney's, GoComics, *and* Angry Asian Man. *Find her cartoons on social media @cartoonconnie.*

RICHIE POPE *(RIH-chee POPE) is a cartoonist and illustrator from Newport News, Virginia. His illustrations have been recognized by* Society of Illustrators, Spectrum, *and* American Illustration, *and his comics have been published by* Shortbox *and* Youth in Decline. *His short comic "That Box We Sit On" was awarded an Ignatz Award for Outstanding Artist. He lives with his partner and their cat in Dallas, Texas. You can find him online at richiepope.com and @richiepope.*

This book was acquired by Weslie Turner, edited by Kait Feldmann, and designed by Baily Crawford. The production was supervised by Melissa Schirmer. The text was set in Georgia, with display type set in Burford Rustic Line and Blackout. The book was printed and bound at LSC Communications in Crawfordsville, Indiana. The manufacturing was supervised by Angelique Browne.